'I am delighted to have app Gokhale's new novel, *Jaip* backdrop of the wonderful Ja utterly charmed by the engro use of my poetry very apt a within stories about the inner life of writers very moving. I particularly enjoyed encountering the burglar- poet Raju Srivastav 'Betaab'' **Javed Akhtar**

'There's more to life than books," says a character in Namita Gokhale's delightful novel. And the author proceeds to demonstrate just that with her multiple tales of love and longing, yearnings and disappointments, unfolding against the backdrop of the teeming Jaipur Literary Festival. Funny, insightful, mordant, and moving in turn. An unalloyed pleasure!' **Shashi Tharoor**

'Namita Gokhale gives us the ultimate insider's view on the "greatest literary show on Earth," the Jaipur Literary Festival. *Jaipur Journals* is a clear-eyed, funny, and poignant rendering of literary ambition and the longing for recognition. You'll be compelled to turn the pages, and by the end you will understand something essential about writers' commitment to their craft, about heartbreak and failure and success' **Vikram Chandra**

'Namita Gokhale's new novel is a literary laugh riot, which is sure to send the book world into a mad rush to unscramble who is who!' **Meena Kandasamy**

Jaipur Journals

Namita Gokhale

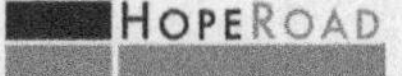

HopeRoad Publishing
PO Box 55544
Exhibition Road
London SW7 2DB

www.hoperoadpublishing.com

First published by Penguin Random House India 2019
This edition first published by HopeRoad in 2021

Javed Akhtar's poem 'Fairs' reproduced with permission from *In Other Words* by Javed Akhtar, published by HarperCollins, India

A CIP catalogue record for this book is available from the British Library

ISBN: 978-1-913109-80-6
eISBN: 978-1-913109-14-1

Printed and bound by Clays Ltd, Elcograf S.p.A

Dedicated to the Jaipur Literature Festival,
and to all the untold stories in the world.

Jaipur

To Jaipur, January

The train to Jaipur. As it hurtles along the track, twelve-year-old Anura observes the woman on the seat opposite her. She is old, as old as Anura is young. She has fallen asleep, and her head tilts over to one side, almost falling off her neck, like a nearly decapitated doll or a broken lampshade.

She makes low, whistling sounds as she snores. Her long white hair is loosely braided and tied up into a bun by what looks like a knitting needle. The train table in front of her is crowded with her two bags - a large leather handbag and a canvas one with a wooden handle.

Outside, the dawn is breaking on fields of mustard. Hills that look like the humps of ancient dromedaries stand silhouetted against the faint first flush of the morning sky.

The lady gets up to go to the toilet. She picks up both the bags, then puts the canvas one back down on the table. She stares at Anura for a while, then speaks to her in a voice that is surprisingly animated. 'Will you watch this bag for me, please?' she asks. 'It's very precious to me but I can't carry it into the toilet.'

Anura nods her head vigorously but doesn't say anything. She likes to save up her words for important things. She watches the lady teeter towards the wc in the rear of the carriage. At one point she almost trips over her purple shawl, but then rights herself.

Anura is looking out of the window when the strange woman returns. 'Thank you kindly, mademoiselle,' the woman says, rummaging through the canvas bag as she speaks, as though to make sure the contents are still safe.

'You are welcome, ma'am,' Anura responds politely.

'And what takes you to Jaipur?' the woman continues. 'Are you travelling alone?'

'It's just a school trip, ma'am, and I have friends in the compartment with me,' Anura replies. As a rule, she discourages curiosity, and has grown up resisting the questions of older people. Her name is Anuradha, but she has shortened it to Anura. It is a school trip, but not just any old school trip. She and her friend Farhan have been selected for a Young Adult session at the Greatest Literary Show on Earth. She is going to read a chapter - a very short chapter - from her book of dystopian fiction that she has self-published on Amazon. It is about a schoolteacher who goes mad. It has a surprise ending, and Anura will make sure she does not give it away when she reads from the book. Anura never gives anything away.

Farhan, a boy from her school but three years older, has won a blogging competition. The pair are travelling with a teacher and six other students to learn about books and writers.

Anura wonders what the canvas bag contains. Perhaps it's contraband? Her mind starts searching for stories about the bag. Some of them are utterly implausible, but her novelist's mind already understands that to sound real, a story must also be fantastic, and that the merely ordinary is not always convincing.

She decides that the bag contains a snake, a rare species of snake, a poisonous one that has been defanged. The old lady is carrying it for her nephew, who lives in Jaipur and is doing research on reptiles and artificial intelligence. Snakes, especially cobras, have photographic memories, and the young nephew requires samples. The canvas bag with its wooden handle contains a cobra, or maybe two, which the lady has stolen from a zoo. Perhaps one of the snakes has not been defanged properly …

Anura likes the way the story is unfolding. She studies the bag, watching out for any squirming movements within that might confirm her theory, but there are none.

Lulled by the rhythmic movement of the train, she dozes off and awakens to find that they have arrived at Jaipur Junction railway station. Farhan is standing beside her, urging her to get up. The lady in the seat opposite is trying to gather up her shawl, her handbag and her canvas tote bag, and is making a mess of it.

'Can I help you with your things, ma'am?' Anura asks courteously, and picks up the canvas bag. She doesn't think her story could be true, but the excitement of the tale has got to her.

The bag is heavy, and there is no movement within. She manages a peep inside as the passengers push and tumble, and sees a thick sheaf of spiral-bound papers. She is both exhilarated and disappointed. Could this person be a writer?

And then the lady takes the bag back from her and clasps it tightly.

Once outside, the momentum of the crowds on the platform takes over. Anura forgets the lady with the canvas bag and the story she has woven around her, although one day she will remember and recognise that face again.

Jaipur, January, Thursday

Around her, the sounds of the lit-fest, of hissing microphones and frenzied footfalls and occasional bursts of applause. In her heart, poison and vitriol. In her canvas bag, her unpublished magnum opus, entitled *UNSUBMITTED.*

Rudrani Rana's hands trembled as she worked painstakingly on her notes. There was a word she had heard today for the first time. She knew a lot about words and their meanings - English words, not these desi, khichdi pidgin languages. Yet she had never encountered this one.

'I am *not* a troglodyte!' Shashi Tharoor had asserted in his session, which was quite predictably the most crowded in the festival so far. Rudrani had found a perch in the long corridor near the press terrace - one of the few benefits accorded to senior citizens.

Troglodyte. Now what could that be? Tharoor had tried to explain it, but his words had been drowned in cheers and applause.

'Rudrani is a walking dictionary, a two-legged thesaurus!' her schoolteacher and mentor Stella Murch had declared, in those long-ago days when she had been young. Her salad days.

Rudrani's varicose veins were acting up and her feet were hurting. She began searching for her well-thumbed pocket dictionary.

Troglodyte: noun (especially in prehistoric times)

- a person who lives in a cave

- a hermit

- a person who is regarded as being deliberately ignorant or old-fashioned

'Hmphh,' she said to herself. She enjoyed hmphhing to herself. It was a form of expression both ironic and self-deprecatory, and it helped voice her very real frustrations with life as she was living it.

Hmphh, grr, gosh, golly - words she had learned and cherished at boarding school in Dehradun. She had been a day scholar at the Waverley Girls School. Not living there with the other girls had been a great handicap and disadvantage, and these expressions had been derived only second-hand, from the boarding-school novels she had borrowed from the lending library in Rajpur Road. A schoolgirl in one of these treasured novelettes was in the habit of exclaiming, 'Hurrah and jolly hockey sticks!' Rudrani Rana's thirteen-year-old self had been enchanted by the phrase. 'Hurrah and jolly hockey sticks!' She would practise the words before the mirror, or whisper them to herself sometimes. She didn't play hockey, or lacrosse, which sounded even more mysterious and alluring. She was in the school kho-kho team, clearly not in the same league of sports.

It was an advantage that her mother was the matron at Waverley; it meant they didn't have to pay regular fees, and they could lodge in the staff quarters. But it made the girl unpopular, even though her kind, efficient mother was a firm favourite with junior and senior classes alike.

Mrs Rana was an institution unto herself, but her daughter Rudrani was considered 'odd'. It was a damning adjective, and she never got over it. 'Odd Rudi' ... that's what she had remained. Well, great writers were supposed to be eccentric, weren't they?

So here she was, with 135,000 words, handwritten in sloping italics and stored in a canvas bag with wooden handles. *UNSUBMITTED* - or, to use its working title, *The Face by the Window*. Unsubmitted. Unseen and unread. Seventeen drafts. Brutal revisions. Discarded chapters. Characters exiled and obliterated. Fates rewritten. Consequences undone.

The novel was dedicated to Alice Walker and *The Color Purple*. She had seen the film before she read the book. Celine. Oprah Winfrey. Whoopi Goldberg. The book felt like an old friend - a pen friend she had finally got to meet. The film, the book, Alice Walker, had released her from that burden of guilt and pain that lay coiled in her heart and her womb.

She had scribbled notes in the margins of the pages, read and reread the book until the spine of the paperback had given way and cracked up. Rudrani had got it bound again, to hold the pages together as they held her together.

The Color Purple. She always wore something purple, after she saw the film. Always.

It was the lure of meeting Oprah Winfrey that had drawn her to the Jaipur Festival that first time in 2012. This was her third year now, and she knew her way around the crowds; she knew how to find a seat and hold on to it; she knew how to tell the speakers what she thought of them, how to debunk their hubris, bring them back down to earth.

Oprah had lived up to Rudrani's every expectation, even though being there meant that Rudrani's feet had been trampled over by a herd of demented fans. When asked about her first response to India, Oprah had said: '… it seems a bit chaotic, but there is an underlying calm and flow.'

That's what it was like with her novel, with *UNSUBMITTED*. It had been in its eighth or ninth draft at that point. It was chaotic, there was no doubt it was chaotic, but it had an underlying calm and flow. It was almost as though Oprah Winfrey had understood the essence of Rudrani's book, was speaking *about* her book, when she had said those words to Barkha Dutt.

In the years to come, all the way to the seventeenth and final draft, she had held on to Oprah's words like a mantra. It was that underlying calm and flow that she had aimed to achieve through every arduous rewrite. Was that word really the best, most appropriate one? Was that adjective superfluous? Should she grant the reader more space, more perspective, to be able to understand the story on its own terms?

So it continued, year after year. The same story told and retold, characters renamed, characters changing their gender, their ages recalculated to fit into the chronology. Rudrani went about disguising them, liberating them, sometimes killing them, and on occasion bringing them back to life.

The people she met in daily life were distant shadows, viewed through a filter. Figures on a stage, characters within an untold plot, protagonists in an unfolding narrative.

In *UNSUBMITTED/The Face by the Window* she had told her story, she was done with it, and all that remained of her resided in those crowded pages.

Only the first line had never been changed or revised: *My body remains a haunted house.*

Unknown to Rudrani Rana, a bearded young man, seated nearby in the crowded press terrace, was observing her keenly as she sat hunched over her notes, pondering the past, contemplating the meaning of the word troglodyte.

He had sketched her with quick and cruel accuracy - the finely sculpted features, the slight hunch, the unravelling bun, the trailing shawl. He had noted and included the two bags, the leather one and the canvas tote.

Anirban M. had an aged aunt in Kolkata who looked like this lady. His heart flowed over with an unexpected surge of compassion. He resolved to be kind to her.

'I'm Anirban M.,' he said, 'and I'm a graphic artist. I've made a sketch of you, and I was wondering if you might sign it for me?'

'Oh, really?' she responded, quite flustered to be engaging in a real conversation. 'I don't know what to say! I'm just an old troglodyte, really …'

He raised an eyebrow and smiled, as though they were sharing a delicious private joke.

Something within her gave way, melted in the warmth of his smile. 'I'm Rudrani Rana,' she said, 'and I'm a failed novelist. I write anonymous letters. To signal to the world what I am thinking. To let them know.'

He was amused, intrigued. There was spunk in this woman, she had surprises.

'Do you sign them "The Troglodyte"?' he asked.

'That's enough information for now, young man,' she told him, casting her lips into what she hoped was an enigmatic smile. 'No one knows this in the world but you.'

Anirban smiled back, displaying a set of even, nicotine-stained teeth, and a disarming dimple on his left cheek. 'Well, I suppose I'm a sort of secret agent too,' he declared, his eyes sparkling with mischief. 'I write - and draw - a graphic column for *New Delhi Times*. You may have come across it - it's called *Eye Spye*. I'm here as a speaker, but I'm always searching for stories that remain hidden to the more jaded eye.'

'Behold! We share a secret,' she responded. 'Charmed to meet you, Anirban M. We shall doubtless bump into each other again. And I too shall deny this conversation if you decide to out me.'

She struggled to gather together her shawl, her hair, her bags, and walked out regally, purposefully.

Anirban M. watched her theatrical departure, the near-tragic bathos of her stumbling steps. His occasional column, *Eye Spye* carried pen sketches and wry observations about all that he encountered. Rudrani Rana was an outsider too. He understood and respected that.

Anirban M. was born Anirban Mukerjee. He grew up in the innards of an extended joint family. They lived in Patna, in an old three-storey house near the Bankipore Club, off the Judges Court Road. The top floor, where he had grown up with his widowed mother, had a view of the distant Ganga as it snaked through the mud banks and dilapidated ghats.

Everything in him, everything that he stood for, all that he rebelled against, had its roots in that house, that room, those days. 'The joint family is the default mode of the Indian psyche,' he had declared, in a youthfully pretentious essay written for his college magazine.

Their joint family, headed by his mother's uncle, had eighteen members living together, eating together. His mother had been a rebel in her time; she had run away and had a 'love marriage' with a young fellow student. The fact that Anirban's father had been a fellow Brahmin, that she had not challenged the barriers of caste, had softened the blow somewhat.

His father had died when Anirban was two. He had been travelling in a bus that had fallen off a bridge into the monsoon-swollen waters of the flooding Ganga. The body had never been recovered.

His mother had returned in distress to her parental home, and been assigned the tiny room on the top floor with its partial view of the river. She got a job as a teacher in a nearby school and devoted herself to her son, ignoring the taunts and minor cruelties that inevitably came her way as someone situated at the bottom of the complex hierarchy of the joint family.

The river was very important to Anirban as he grew up, the sacred river that had swallowed up his father. The family house had been a happy home in its way, full of feasts and festivities, always crowded with visiting relatives. His mother's uncle was a lawyer with a flourishing practice. He was unfailingly kind to Anirban, and as considerate as the constraints of his busy life could allow.

But Anirban always felt marked: he felt different, an outlier, an outsider. Even as a schoolchild he was always enacting minor rebellions, to establish that his strangeness was wilful, that he was master of his own otherness.

There was the time he had shaved off his hair, even the residual topknot that proclaimed his Brahminical status. He had still been in school then, in the eleventh grade. His mother had covered up for him at home by announcing that his curly locks had been infested by lice. 'There is a dirty and badly brought up boy who sits next to him in class,' she explained to her uncle. 'We had to shave his hair to get rid of the lice. I have requested the class teacher to change his seat.'

But in private she reproached Anirban and wept at his transgressions, quiet tears which she did not hide from him.

It was his aunt from Kolkata who had sorted him out. She would share their room when she visited them in Patna, in the house near Judges Court Road and the Bankipore Club.

She was his uncle's cousin, really, and his mother's cousin-aunt, but he always thought of her as his Mashi-ma. She had been taller than any of the women that he knew, and reed thin. Her cotton saris were tied high and ended just above her ankles; they were woven for a shorter, more compliant woman. She wore a pair of shell-shaped gold earrings, a battered watch, and two thin gold bangles on her wrists. No other ornaments: no bindi on her forehead, no mangal sutra around her neck. She was a widow like his mother, but a hardier breed of survivor.

'People behave with you as you allow them to behave,' she had told him once. 'Weave an invisible cloak, like Mr India in that movie. Remember it's all a game. Step back a little and they will stay out of your way too.' She had said this in a casual, offhand way, apropos of nothing in particular, but it had reached out to him with all the force of a guru mantra, a commandment from the heavens that he accepted with gratitude.

Everything had fallen into place after that. The scholarship to Berlin, the awards, the graphic books - everything had been a natural, painless progression once he had stepped back, watching the world as though through a glass window.

Something about Rudrani Rana reminded him of his Mashi-ma. He understood her vulnerability, recognised her pain, respected her strength.

What would he write about her? She too was essentially an outlier, looking on wistfully at the charmed circle of celebrity and success on parade. He wondered about her novel and her poison-pen letters, and what had led her to confide in him about them. And what indeed had led him to share his well-guarded identity with her.

He set out for the next session, marked with a fluorescent gel pen on his carefully annotated programme: an Icelandic writer was to read from her new novel and discuss 'Nordic Noir and Environmental Crime'. There were two publishers' parties after that, and a flagrant invitation from an attractive journalist who had made him aware of her polyamorous tendencies. He was cautious about women now, and would prudently let the invitation pass.

Rudrani Rana had returned to her clean and quiet room in a nearby guesthouse. She had planned to read through *UNSUBMITTED* once more, but now decided against it.

'Too many revisions,' she told herself. 'It's becoming an echo chamber.'

She turned instead to other writers, reading, as was her habit, two books at a time: *The Moving Finger* by Agatha Christie and *The Prime of Miss Jean Brodie* by Muriel Spark. She had underlined passages from *The Moving Finger* and the pages had comments in the margins. Always with a pencil, never a pen.

Why? she asked herself. Why had she written her own book? Why had she spent a lifetime brooding over this story, adding to and deleting from it, rendering it all but unrecognisable as hers? Except in the substance, except in the details, even as she tried out more and more disguises, different pitches of ventriloquist voices.

X was surely her mother. Rudrani had given her protruding teeth and a horsey laugh when Mrs Rana, beloved matron of the Waverley Girls School, had in fact a pronounced underbite. This made her appear rather modest and refined. When she laughed, which was not often, it would sound as though she was swallowing or stifling her laughter, and when she spoke, she had a way of tucking her chin into her neck so as not to trap her words into her misaligned teeth - to somehow cough them out and set them free.

The buck teeth and bellowing laugh were enough, Rudrani felt, to hide from the world that X was actually her mother. In any case, Mrs Rana had been dead for many decades now. She had been cremated, not buried, for she was after all a Hindu wife. All that remained of her was a steel trunk with her name embossed on it, and the mildewed papers and photographs within it. And a long black cardigan that had kept its shape and which Rudrani still wore, sometimes, without sentimentality.

And what of Y? Y was Rupert Murch, so true to life that the character lacked the freedom of fiction. She had written him without artifice, drawing from her heart. From her broken heart, now immured by the telling and retelling of that hurt. His story was like a scab, an armament against past and future pain.

In her novel, it was she who broke his heart. In consequence, Rupert had set off on a ship to Australia, leaving behind all that he loved and cared for, to build up a new life. Towards the end of the narrative, the reader encountered him, still handsome, but stooped and melancholy, his hair now grey, but still long and curly as she remembered it.

Rupert was not the hero of *UNSUBMITTED*, nor was he the villain. He was strong and he was weak and, Rudrani had concluded, in the final analysis, he was pathetic. A man who was afraid of his mother.

Y's mother was the paradox of the piece, the character who broke through her boundaries to become the central figure in this story of interrelated lives. Z - based on Stella Murch - overturned the very terms of the disdain and dislike with which she had been conceived and became almost the central figure of the tale, with a triumphant life all her own.

And Rudrani Rana? She was in the shadow of every line, of every vexed question, part of every hope and despair and consolation.

My body remains a haunted house.

What would happen if her book was published? And read by others? She would have revealed herself, made herself naked. No, she assured herself, *UNSUBMITTED* would remain just that, her private masterpiece, all the more precious for being hidden from the world.

Quentin Cripps sneezed. It was a long, violent sneeze, and it shook him up. The interminable flights had taken their toll. New York to Heathrow to Mumbai to Jaipur. He looked for his blue checked handkerchief but it was not to be found.

Why on earth had they called him here, to this carnival, to speak about Walt Disney? Minnie Mouse had travelled the globe and the history of Mickey Mouse was available in Hindi translation, but he was still unsure about how to position his talk. It was to be a conversation with an Indian lady with a tongue-twister of a name, a graphic artist who wrote about popular culture.

The green room was partly open to the sky, covered with multi-coloured drapes. It had an unfamiliar smell, of incense and marigolds and strong coffee. He located the handkerchief - it was in his iPad case - and blew his nose resoundingly into it.

Zoya Mankotia was reading her notes, preparing for her session. She turned to him in alarm. 'I hope you are all right?' she asked. She didn't need to borrow any germs.

He sneezed again, not so loudly this time. 'Sorry about that!' he exclaimed. 'Must be something I picked up on the flight. Maybe I should go and sit in the sunshine for a while.' He walked out of the authors' lounge into the dazzling winter light, and had a cup of masala chai. The taste of cinnamon and cardamom and ginger had a magical effect on his respiratory system. The tea was brewing in an enormous burnished-copper pot, poured out into an earthen cup with a long steel scoop. It was almost mystical.

The man who was pouring the tea had a fierce moustache which curved and curled around his face. He wore a red and yellow turban, and looked like a warrior. Nothing could be more different from New York or Somerset. And yet, oddly, Quentin felt more at home here than he had ever done before, anywhere in the world.

He counted all the places he had lived in through the spectrum of forty-five years. Somerset in the west of England. Poughkeepsie in New York State. Nepal. Bangkok. Sri Lanka. Somalia. Zambia. Pakistan. London. Ireland, where he spent a year trying to complete his first novel. The novel that never got written.

Three fathers, two of them adoptive. Two mothers, one of them biological. Eleven countries, observed through the Peace Corps, and war journalism. It had been like living in a scrapbook full of disconnected memories. Memories that didn't add up or hold together. And yet he felt at home here, amidst this ocean of strangers, speaking in a babel of languages he understood and didn't understand, multitudes of people all in search of something.

It had been an unlikely trajectory, across the passionate convictions of his parents and surrogate parents, and his own passions and disappointments. Nothing in his life, no phase or aspect of it, had ever led logically from one part to another.

And here he was, in India, presenting his wildly successful biography of Walt Disney. *Disney and the American Dream*.

Walt Elias Disney. Born 5 December 1901 in Hermosa, Chicago. The man who was representative of an age, the entrepreneurial equal of Ford and Edison, the icon of American ingenuity, imagination and free enterprise.

Like everything else, Walt Disney had entered Quentin's life by accident. Quentin had gone to Segovia, partly to research an article he was assembling for a literary magazine. It was about Ernest Hemingway and his journeys in Spain to cover the civil war for the North American Newspaper Alliance. *For Whom the Bell Tolls* was written three years later.

Quentin had travelled through the Sierra de Guadarrama, examining the remains of bunkers, dugouts and trenches. When he reached Segovia he fell in love with the town and its Roman aqueducts, and indeed with a young woman he encountered there. It was perhaps no coincidence that she was named Maria, like the heroine of Hemingway's novel.

That time in Segovia had led Quentin Cripps to Disney. The Alcazar de Segovia, with its grey slate towers and turrets topped with witches-hat roofs, had been the inspiration for the prototype fairy-tale castle of Disney lore, of Cinderella and Snow White and Rapunzel. It was there that Quentin had first kissed Maria, on a warm summer's day. It had another even more important influence and consequence. His biography of Walt Disney, begun on a lighthearted impulse, had been the first and only major success in his life.

Ernest Hemingway was born in Oak Park, just west of Chicago, Illinois, on 21 July 1899. A year and a half before Walt Disney and yet they were divided by a century.

Quentin warmed himself in the sun. The sneezing had stopped. He got himself another cup of masala chai and listened in to the sounds of Hindi and English and Spanish - some Nepali too - around him. Language could be soothing when it reduced itself to sound waves, when words lost their particularity and became vibrations.

He tried to focus on his session. How would he craft it for the motley crowds at Jaipur? 'It was all started by a mouse ...' that was how his usual presentation began, with a video clip of a debonair Walt Disney telling the tale. He would work on it and position it for India, somehow, after meeting with his interlocutor Ms Complicated Long Name that he couldn't remember.

He was overtaken by a wave of jet lag, and the sensory overload didn't help. He settled down on a vacant chair in a session in progress on the Front Lawn. A Frenchman with a pronounced accent and a quartet of women were arguing about something. He recognised one of them from the authors' lounge - the striking-looking woman with a mane of grey hair who had asked if he was all right.

He checked the name of the meeting in the festival brochure. It was called 'The Second Sex'. The panel was quarrelling about feminism. He was tired of sessions on gender - in fact, they annoyed him, in so many big and small ways. He was not homophobic, he told himself, or a misogynist. He liked to think he was sensitive to women's needs. But he was a man's man. He valued his masculinity: that, after all, was what had drawn him to Hemingway.

Quentin Cripps had stopped paying any attention to the speakers. He was listening to the spool playing inside his own head.

What had gone wrong with the world? The new dictionaries of desire puzzled him, frightened him. Sexuality was an iceberg, only one-ninth of it above water. Pan-sexual. Bisexual. Gender fluid, non-binary, intersex. He would be ticked cisgender, he supposed. And the angry online incels – self-styled 'involuntary celibates' - in the lonely manosphere. Terminologies and labels. Where were the people hiding, where had the tenderness gone?

Then there were exclusions within exclusions: TERFs, SWERFs. 'Dykes not dicks.' The words buzzed in his head like troubled wasps. There was so much to keep up with. This whole thing was turning into anarchy. A hornet's nest.

What place was there here for a straight white man with a broken heart? All he wanted was to hold his woman and be loved by her. Was there a complicated term for that too?

The audience around him was young, much younger than the median age of most festivals he had attended. There was an older woman sitting next to him. She was trying to ask a question, raising her hand agitatedly to get the attention of the people on stage. Her straggly white bun was coming undone and falling all over her face.

He couldn't take any more of it. Standing up, he made his way through the crowds to return to his hotel.

The panel on 'The Second Sex' was in full swing. It consisted of a French-Algerian writer, a radical gender-fluid diaspora novelist, a sexual rights activist, a gentleman from the French Book Office, and an elderly lady from Kolkata who had translated Simone de Beauvoir into Bangla but hadn't yet been allowed to say anything.

'One is not born, but rather becomes, a woman,' Monsieur Didier St Roch concluded with a Gallic shrug. He turned to the other speakers. His brief was to introduce them and keep time.

Zoya Mankotia picked up the hand mic, even though she had been wired up. Her recent novel, *The Quilt*, had created waves, occasioning both outrage and intense appreciation. Her voice held a mélange of accents, and sounded somehow contrived.

'I am a novelist,' she announced, 'and I am as passionate about gender fluidity as I am about crossover genres. I am bi-curious, and yet committed equally to my writing, my primary reason for being, and my wife, my primary partner in a loyal relationship. We can be who we are, write as we like.'

Geetha Gopalan picked up the gauntlet. 'I would like to quote Madame Simone de Beauvoir,' she declaimed forcefully, with the mic held too close to her mouth. Her gentle booming voice created a reverb as she read from *The Second Sex* about the abandonment needed in order for women to enjoy sex. She let that sink in. Then, taking another very deep breath which swept like a breeze through the audience, she spoke of love and the different interpretations of it from both sexes - and how this led to serious misunderstandings.

Simone de Beauvoir's Bangla translator Shonali Sen made a play for the mic. But as she fumbled with the folds of her sari and pulled up the sleeves of her thick hand-knitted cardigan, Leila Nafeesi jumped in and took hold of the conversation.

'What I want to ask you is this,' she said. 'How many of us remember Simone de Beauvoir's seminal work, *The Ethics of Ambiguity*?'

Zoya Mankotia snatched the mic from Leila Nafeesi. 'I want you to withdraw that!' she hissed. 'I demand that you expunge the inappropriate and insensitive use of the word seminal! Words have power. They have responsibility. They have meaning.'

Nafeesi ignored her and continued valiantly, although there was a slight quaver to her voice: 'Simone de Beauvoir's *seminal* work, *The Ethics of Ambiguity*, was overshadowed by the phenomenal success of *The Second Sex* by the entirely patriarchal character of the philosophical canon, and by her being considered as a mere acolyte of Jean-Paul Sartre.'

Zoya Mankotia was fuming, and her grey and black tresses had fallen loose of the band that held them in place. 'Will you kindly withdraw the use of the word seminal?' she said, trying to gain control over herself.

Leila Nafeesi raised an eyebrow, gently, as though in slow motion. 'I am puzzled, Madam Mankotia,' she said. 'If you speak of gender fluidity with such conviction, how can you disallow me the use of this word, this gendered and fluid word, this innocent semen?'

Shonali Sen re-entered the fray. Her voice was clear and articulate. 'The word for semen in Bangla is *Birya*. In Hindi, it is *Virya*. In French, it is *sperme*, although seminal remains *séminal*. The words have very different contexts and connotations. I request you not to get agitated.'

It was getting riotous. Didier St Roch looked at the timer: there were ten minutes to go. The strikingly beautiful Australian venue manager gave him the signal to move to the audience for questions.

'I am afraid our time is up,' he said. 'I wish it was not so, as this is an important conversation on biology, sexual identity and linguistic usage. Any questions from the audience?'

Two hands shot up in the front row. A young girl in a school uniform. An older woman with a mess of white hair tied up in a straggly bun. Her face carried the vestiges of once classic beauty.

'Ma'am! Ma'am!' the young girl said, seizing the mic, a note of extreme urgency in her voice. 'My question is about the politics of menstruation. Why does society expect us to feel guilty about the biology of bleeding?'

'Who would like to answer that?' Didier St Roch asked. The panellists looked at each other questioningly and Zoya Mankotia responded.

'The point about patriarchy - the *key* point about patriarchy ...' The sound system screeched violently and sputtered to a halt. She continued undaunted, but the audience couldn't hear her any more.

'We can't hear you,' the listeners responded. The schoolgirl was listening patiently, but her smile was getting fixed.

The audio coughed back to life. '... the economics of sanitary pads,' Zoya continued sombrely, and then again an electronic screech and silence as she opened and closed her mouth where she was seated, high on the dais.

A parrot swooped across the stage, like a daring trapeze artist. A peahen seated on the low branch of a mango tree let out its harsh call. A tattered yellow kite, impaled against the mango tree, fluttered in the gentle afternoon breeze. And then a monkey appeared, jumping from the highest balcony to the next, and then almost onto the stage.

The audience was taking in these sights. Zoya Mankotia was speaking still, but again, nobody could hear her. The stage manager was gesticulating, indicating that the session had to close. Just then the sound system resuscitated and roared back to life.

'And that's all I have to say,' Zoya Mankotia concluded firmly.

Didier St Roch was at the podium. 'Thank you, ladies and gentlemen, for being with us at this session on the uniquely magnificent and significant French intellect, Simone de Beauvoir,' he said. 'Before I close, I would also like to address the meaningful question presented by the young lady in the front row. I am a man, I do not bleed from the womb, but I would very much like to quote Madame de Beauvoir …'

But before he could finish, the venue manager walked to the podium and addressed the audience. 'On behalf of *She* magazine and all our other sponsors, I would like to thank Ms Geetha Gopalan, Ms Leila Nafeesi, Ms Zoya Mankotia, Ms Shonali Sen, and our able moderator, Monsieur Didier St Roch.'

The members of the distinguished panel rose from their chairs and smiled politely at each other as they picked up their belongings and readied themselves to depart the stage. All except Zoya Mankotia, who strode to the mic and began speaking.

'I will not leave the stage,' she declared, 'until this ridiculous Frenchman apologises for daring to mansplain my menstrual blood, my vital force!'

Didier St Roch judged the situation astutely. 'Madame Zoya, you have my profound apologies. I was only quoting another woman, a woman I admire, but if you object, I withdraw my comment.'

The older woman still had her hand up in the air. She wanted to ask a question, but they had all left the stage by now, all except Shonali Sen, the French-to-Bangla translator of Simone de Beauvoir.

'I too have some last words,' Rudrani Rana said, as she stood on tiptoe to speak into the mic. 'Biology is sometimes destiny. In Mahasweta Devi's great book, *Breast Stories*, the breast is a metaphor for, a metaphor for …'

But speakers for the next panel were already walking up, and the audiences were scattering and reassembling. 'The female breast is more than a metaphor; it is indeed the symbol of an exploitative social system!' she ended triumphantly. She tripped on her sari as she was walking out, and had to be helped to her feet and led away.

In the authors' lounge, the women sat together and continued their conversation. 'The cheek of that man!' Zoya Mankotia exclaimed.

Shonali Sen joined them and Leila Nafeesi made room for her in their circle of chairs. She bent forward to admire the folds of the older woman's batik-printed sari. 'Is it easy to walk around draped in six yards of silk?' she asked wonderingly.

A sense of womanly well-being sat over them.

'I wear saris most of the time,' Zoya said. 'Only handloom and organic cotton. And so does my wife, though she is not an ethnic Indian.' She was dressed today in a white khadi kurta with a blue quilted jacket.

'I am only truly comfortable in a sari,' Geetha Gopalan commented. 'Although I wear trousers when I am travelling in the US.'

A volunteer with a round smooth face and dark shining eyes stepped forward to address the group. 'Please excuse me,' she said, 'but which of you is Ms Zoya Mankotia?'

Zoya swished her mane of grey-flecked hair and lifted one grey-black eyebrow in interrogation. 'You mean me?' she asked, almost girlishly.

'One of your fans was waiting for you. He left this card which he wanted delivered to you,' the smooth-faced volunteer said. 'And I must tell you, Ms Mankotia, that I too am a great fan of yours. I would love you to sign a copy of *The Quilt* for me.'

She handed over a pale purple envelope, with Zoya Mankotia's name written on it with a purple marker in a neat italic hand. Inside was a card with a photograph of a kitten wearing a purple ribbon around its neck.

The message was written in capital letters, in purple ink. It was brief and brutal. 'Miaow, miaow, Ms Mankotia,' it said. 'I can see through you. You faithless bich. I know what you have been up to, how many women you have betrayed. What's more, your pathetic intellectual pretenshuns leave me speechless! And your novel, *The Quilt*, is a copycat version of Ismat Chughtai's *Lihaf*. You plagiarizer, you pornographer ... Your time is up.'

Zoya's expression did not change when she read this, although the set of her jaw tightened visibly. She put the card back into the purple envelope and passed it wordlessly to Geetha Gopalan.

'So who is this mysterious fan?' Geetha asked in her jolly booming voice. 'May I read it?'

Zoya nodded. Geetha Gopalan opened the envelope. 'What on earth is this?' she asked in surprise.

'It is an anonymous letter,' Zoya replied, lifting first one eyebrow, and then the other. 'Or an anonymous card, to be accurate, a deeply critical pretty kitty card.'

'An antediluvian troll,' Geetha Gopalan responded. 'What a nasty man he must be!'

'He could be a woman,' Shonali Sen ventured. The card had been circulated to her and Leila Nafeesi as well.

'I can never make out if men hate women more, or women themselves,' Zoya Mankotia said.

'Purple is a woman's colour, somehow,' Geetha Gopalan observed thoughtfully.

'Oh, please don't get into these tired gender stereotypes,' Zoya snapped, her voice combining weariness and anger.

Leila Nafeesi had been quiet all this while. She spread out her fingers to display her long nails, which were painted purple. She had beautiful, pale ivory hands with rings set in silver on all her fingers - lapis lazuli, turquoise, jade, topaz. 'The colour purple,' she mused. 'By the way, I don't believe someone with such an elegant italic handwriting doesn't know how to spell - it's a pose.'

Just then, Didier St Roch came up to the group. 'Thank you, ladies, for a wonderful panel!' he exclaimed effusively.

They showed him the card. 'But this is a monstrosity,' he reacted agitatedly. 'Of course you have reported it to the authorities?'

'We shall ask the festival secretariat to investigate,' Geetha Gopalan replied. 'But first let me find the young lady who delivered it to us.'

It was time for the next session. Writers and speakers began shuffling in and out of the room. Words and phrases floated around. 'Discourses', 'the connotation is', 'the universal right to asylum', 'a war against clichés'.

Zoya Mankotia took the purple envelope and put it purposefully into her handbag. She was humming defiantly to herself: *'Meri Behene Maange ... Azaadi.'* My sisters want freedom, my daughter wants freedom.

She wasn't going to let a poison pen letter bother her. It took a lot more than that to get Zoya Mankotia down.

And yet. And yet. Zoya was accustomed to being misunderstood and disliked and yet the card, patently absurd as it was, had unnerved her by its rancour, by the ill-will that rose like a miasma from the sloping italic handwriting.

As a young girl, she had been ambivalent about boys. She was suspicious and hostile of the way they talked, the way they walked, the way they smelt. As an adolescent growing up in a conservative Indian family, Zoya's behaviour was met with a mixture of exasperation and baffled amusement. She loved her father and her brother, and her engineer father humoured her, but her mother would admonish her. 'When you get married, you will have to respect and care for your husband,' she would say.

Things didn't get any better when they moved to America. Zoya had been a rebellious fourteen year old, and became even more of an outsider in this new environment. She was drawn to girls and constantly in the throes of a new girl crush. Her skin colour and academic accomplishments only added to the constant conflict.

Later, in college, she dated a few Indian men, but their sense of entitlement, their natural arrogance, repulsed her. She didn't come out even to herself until her college days. Her natural misandry gave way to fully-fledged ideological feminism, a construct that imparted structure and meaning to her life.

Zoya continued to fall in love, passionately and frequently. She wrote fierce poetry after the style of Sappho. She wrote *The Quilt*. The novel was taken seriously in circles that mattered, and received rapturous reviews and accolades within the queer community. She got married, and settled into domesticity with her wife, but continued to fall in love. The contrarian in her was exhilarated by constantly walking against the wind. This purple-penned nonsense should not even have dented her consciousness. But it had.

The burglar wandered here and there, taking in the sights and sounds around him. He had boarded the train to Jaipur with his mind and heart focused on but two goals. One was to meet India's greatest poet, Janab Javed Akhtar. The other was to cover the cost of the trip through some well-executed burglaries, with a margin to spare.

Raju Srivastava was born in Bijnor, the son of an unsuccessful tailor-master. He had worked with his father for a while, and knew the trade. His father had considered it an art; his hemming was more delicate than an ant's tracks, and he would cut the garments with great precision, after feeling and fondling the fabric this way and that, to understand its flow. There were no bulges or creases in the clothes he sewed, and the hand stitching was minute and meticulous. Their fatal flaw was that the garments were always, but always, too tight. Mahinder Master-ji, his father, always cut the cloth too close, leaving no *gunjaish* or scope for alterations. Raju Srivastava had spent his childhood placating, or trying to placate, angry customers whose clothes did not, could not, fit them. They would threaten father and son, create scenes, and almost always leave without paying.

Mahinder Master-ji would be resignedly philosophical about these episodes, and wear an expression of saintly fortitude. His son Raju would be seething with rage, with his father, with the customer, with the clothes that refused to fit. He took the ignominy of it to heart. The hurled curses were like thunderbolts, the suits and jackets and Nehru-style *bundis* all malevolent conspirators in their constant humiliations.

Raju Srivastava had decided to become a poet. He read them all, Nirala and Dushyant Kumar, Muktibodh and Firaq Gorakhpuri and Faiz Ahmed Faiz. He wrote. His preferred form was the ghazal: seven couplets, with a refrain at the end. He knew the form, he knew the metre. It came to him as naturally as the whirring of the sewing machine and the rhythm of his foot on the pedal.

And here before him was Javed Saheb, the thief of hearts, the legend of the Urdu world. He was explaining the difference between a ghazal, a nazm and a geet. 'A ghazal is like a tin of assorted biscuits,' he said, 'with every *sher*, every two-line couplet, a complete little poem in itself. These are held together, strung together, by virtue of the metre and the rhyme.'

Raju Srivastava listened intently, taking in every single word, every gesture, of his hero. His own *takhallus*, his pen name, was 'Betaab' - the impatient one. And indeed he was *betaab* - impatient to get all that he wanted from life, in a hurry to succeed, somehow, anyhow. But in that moment he was not impatient; he had surrendered himself to the magic of Javed Saheb's voice, and to the transformative world of poetry.

The young man beside him looked like a poet too. He was handsome, in a smooth, rich way, with carefully maintained stubble on his chin and thick locks of curly well-conditioned hair that fell artfully over his forehead, adding an air of drama to his studied persona. As the young man leaned forward to listen all the more intently to Javed Sahib's words of wisdom, a wallet fell out of his pocket onto the dusty grass. Raju Srivastava 'Betaab' bent down to pick it up, his motionless eyes carefully scanning the faces around to see if anyone had noticed. He held the wallet in his hand for a while, casually, and waited for the opportune moment to pocket it. But his intuition, his infallible instincts which had let him down only once, told him that he was being watched, and that he would be caught.

He nudged the young man on the knee and handed the wallet back. 'Thank you, bro!' the young man said, and gave him an unexpected hug. Raju recognised the cologne he was wearing. The young man reached into his wallet and took out an embossed visiting card. 'Thanks, bro,' he said again, 'and that's me.'

Betaab was not a pickpocket. He was proud of his craft. He worked alone and took no hostages. The *Indian Express* had referred to him as the capital's nimblest cat burglar. He thought the accolade well deserved. He had no visiting card to offer in return. '*Dost, main shayar hoon*,' he said in reply. 'I myself am a poet, and a fan of Javed Saheb. I too write Urdu poetry. My pen name is Betaab.'

'*Arre*, Javed-ji is a family friend,' the young man said casually. 'That's why I'm here.'

And now the great poet was reciting some lyric poetry, in Hindustani, and in English translation. It was a long poem, about a village fair.

Fairs

Clutching his father's finger,
when a small child
went to the fair for the first time
his innocent bright eyes
looked on a new world.
'What is this? What is that?'
he asked excitedly.
His father, bending low,
told him the names
of many things, many spectacles;
about the jugglers,
the daredevils,
the conjurors,
and what they did.
Then they turned home.
The child rocked
in the cradle of his father's arms
and rested his head upon his shoulder.
The father asked,
'Are you sleepy?'

Time is like a bird
that keeps flying.
The fair returned to the village.
The old father
clutched his son's arm with trembling hands
while the son
explained all he could
about what this was and what that was.
The father rested his head on his son's shoulder.
The son asked:
'Are you sleepy?'
The father turned,
looked down at the memory lane,
saw the dust kicked up
by moments past,
good ones and bad,
the bitter and the sweet -
and then, turning towards his son,
a faint smile playing on his lips,
said softly,
'Yes! I am sleepy now.'

The audience broke into deafening applause. Betaab found he was weeping uncontrollably. The poem had unearthed a wound within him which had never healed. The young man next to him was looking at him with concern. The rest of the frenzied crowd took no notice.

His father. He had developed cancer, of the lungs. There was no money for the treatment. Mahinder Master-ji, his papa-ji, looked stricken and shamed by his illness and the trouble it was causing his family. It was then that Betaab attempted his first burglary. They were in Lucknow, where his father was receiving daily doses of chemotherapy at the Gandhi Memorial Hospital. They were lodged at his father's cousin's house in Qaiserbagh and overstaying their welcome.

Raju targeted a multistorey building in Sitapur Road. It was a new complex, with the residents still moving in. The security guard was a drunken lad from Gorakhpur. Posing as a carpenter, Betaab went to the flats above and below flat 322, and walked around until he could measure each step in the dark. The flat belonged to a lottery vendor, and Raju was reasonably sure there would be cash lying around. The family had gone to see a film at the multiplex, and the helper had stepped down for a beedi and a chat with the guard.

Raju had made a haul of eleven lakhs, all those years ago when a lakh meant something. Before demonitisation or the introduction of the Goods and Services Tax. He had moved his mother into a three-star hotel; she was too startled and afraid to protest. He had rented a small flat for them after that, and hired a decent part-time help. He had done his duty to his parents, and when they died a year later, within weeks of each other, he had donated a lakh of rupees to an orphanage in their memory. Yes, he had done his duty, repaid his debt to Mahinder Master-ji, and his other debts as well. And if Javed Saheb's poem made him cry, it was a testimony to the power of poetry and the vulnerability of the human heart.

*

The Bhopa, the Rajasthani priest-singer, was reciting the genealogy of his benefactors as his wife, the Bhopi, held up a lamp to illuminate the scroll, the Phad, which was strung up between two bamboo poles. He began on the epic narrative, his voice gravelly, with no need of a megaphone as it resonated across the lawns of the Diggi Palace.

As the evening set on the Jaipur Literature Festival, a granular photographic quality settled upon the crowds. A sari-clad woman with an American accent interrupted the Bhopa to speak about the oral heritage of Rajasthan. 'The bard, Madan Bhopa, belongs to the nomadic Nayaka tribe and employs the Shekhavati dialect to invoke Pabuji, the ascetic deity of the sand desert.

'The physical arrangements of the Phad are integral to understanding the orally transmitted tales. The ten-foot-long scroll is divided into smaller units, each illustrating some form of Pabuji's exploits. It is up to the Bhopa to decide which sub-stories he chooses to link up. Hence each recital is unique in itself and to the particular narrator, to be endlessly retold, as an act of worship within the sacred site of the scroll.'

Rudrani Rana observed the scene around her with an emotion that approached fatigue. There were too many words here, in too many languages, too many tenses. She wanted to get back to her room, to climb into bed, to read a book by the light of the dim bedside lamp.

'These tales of valour, revolving around a medieval Rajput hero, are part and parcel of the cultural heritage of Rajasthan,' the woman concluded.

The Bhopa, in his bardic attire of turban, robe and sash looked weary. The effulgence that had surrounded his ritual performance had worn off. He looked tired, and depressed, and Rudrani's heart went out to him.

The speaker irritated her. She was of a certain type, Rudrani concluded, compounded of intellectual entitlement, and the careless assurance of class, privilege, good looks and an American Green Card.

She looked up the speaker's name in her programme sheet. *Gayatri Smyth Gandhy. Historian and cultural anthropologist*. Rudrani could feel the bile rising within her. She could taste the doughnuts and coffee she had relished just a short while ago. Her fingers trembled with the urge to give vent to her feelings. But she restrained herself. It could wait until she got home.

She extracted a chewable strawberry-flavoured antacid from her capacious handbag, and calmed herself before she set out to find an auto-rickshaw for the journey back.

After a frugal dinner of roti and sabzi, she searched through her suitcase for an appropriate card. She found one of a kitten playing with a ball of purple wool which she decided established the mood she wanted to set. Later, she sat on her bed and composed the letter. It had to be just the right mix of erudition and invective.

'You Bich,' she began, in her preferred mode of address. 'You posturing plagiarist. This is culchural condescension and all-too-typical colonial-style appropriation. Do you even realise that you live off the folk artistes and musicians you talk so glibly about? I wonder what they have to say about *you*. You may think you are so WOKE, but you have no skin in the game!'

Rudrani was particularly proud of the last line. She worked hard to keep up with current vocabulary. 'Woke' was a newly acquired word and she delighted in it.

Woke: verb; adjective INFORMAL US.

- Alert to injustice in society, especially racism.

- 'We need to stay angry, and stay woke.'

That was what she was. A woke troglodyte. She slid the card into her handbag, and settled down to read before she fell asleep.

Jaipur, January, Friday

Rudrani awoke feeling mysteriously rejuvenated. Her legs didn't ache and she felt somehow light and optimistic. Deciding to spend the day in exploration, she set out for the old city, with no particular destination in mind. She would watch out for signs, to guide her on her way.

Along the crowded pavement, a man sat crouched over a parrot in a cage. *Past, present, future. Told and Foretold*, the sign declared. She knelt down to meet the parrot's beady glare. The man asked for two hundred rupees for a reading. They settled for a hundred and fifty.

He laid out the cards and instructed Rudrani to touch them one by one, with the little finger of her right hand, and no other.

'Why?' she asked.

'Never forget, mata-ji, that is where your good luck resides,' he told her.

The cage had *Parrot Tarot* painted in funky gold letters. The bird was let out of its blue iron cage. It hopped around disinterestedly, then began pecking repeatedly at one of the cards.

'Is this the right card, Tota-Raja?' he asked. The parrot flapped its wings and let out a long shrill shriek, and the man picked up the card the parrot had indicated.

'Your name begins with Rrr,' he declared, speaking in Hindi and emphasising the guttural sound of the R. 'What is your name, sister?'

'My name is Rudrani,' she conceded.

'You have been very lonely and unhappy for many, many years.'

What could she say?

The parrot alighted on a second card. The fortune teller began chatting on his mobile phone, scratching his underarms as he spoke.

'This year you will find happiness,' he pronounced, when he was through with his call. 'Bad times over. Good time begins. Fame, fortune and success.'

The parrot looked up at her.

'Ram Ram!' it said, in a strangely masculine timbre. 'Shubh Shubh!' Another shriek. 'Stay Blessed!'

'Stay Blessed' was articulated in an American accent, in a woman's voice. 'Stay Blessed! Stay Blessed! Stay Blessed! Stay Blessed!' The parrot wouldn't, couldn't, stop.

'Two cards only. My fees please,' Ram said politely.

Her legs hurt. She was not accustomed to squatting at ground level. She felt old, and tired, and defeated. She picked up her two bags, and decided to make her way back to the festival.

Gayatri Smyth Gandhy, fifty-two, single, divorced, citizen of the world. Academic and aspiring novelist. Drinking cups of steaming ginger tea and watching the morning sky turn a brilliant blue, listening to the parrots in the neem tree, remembering her childhood in scattered cantonment towns and army outposts across India. Worrying, as she often did, about what her novel was 'about'. The certitudes of plot and structure collapsing in a wallow of self-interrogation. Knowing that she was stuck, and that it was, somewhere, not working.

Her annual pilgrimages home usually found her divided, cleft by the distances between her Indian and Western selves. Gayatri's father, Brig Gandhy, had been stationed in Jaipur for some years. She had lived there, studied there, age eleven to thirteen. She was, in some part, a Jaipurite. This visit had given her something, made her feel a part of the anarchic pandemonium of life in India.

She had planned to work on the synopsis of her novel, to make the intricate plotting accessible in a few beguiling paragraphs. Gayatri studied her notes. 'One of the principal characters in the novel is drawn from Indian mythology. Yama, the Lord of Death, is both a servant and master of fate. The other mythic protagonist in the story is Kama, the God of Love. He is depicted as he is described in the ancient texts, a chubby, pre-pubescent boy shooting arrows of desire, often indiscriminately.' She admired the sentences, felt justifiably proud of the innovative and contemporary way in which she had handled the fuzzy edges of mythic reality.

Gayatri made her way to the festival grounds in the Diggi Palace. The crowds were jostling and shoving in a collective high of celebrity fever and literary fervor. She took the shortcut she had discovered from behind the stage to the speakers' lounge and scanned the room for company. A famous African-American writer, a longstanding contender for the Nobel, was sneezing violently, and a festival volunteer was offering him a box of tissues. A Rajasthani writer, in a magnificent multi-coloured turban, stood surrounded by a gaggle of admirers. There were a few other familiar-unfamiliar faces. And then her heart stopped as she saw *him*, her first-ever lover, prime among the three men to have sequentially broken her heart.

Sumedh Kumar had not seen her. He was absorbed in deep conversation with an auburn-haired woman. Gayatri knew she was his second wife. His first wife, her once best friend, sociologist turned travel writer Anita Husain, had been dumped some years ago. As she herself had been.

The heart has its reasons of which reason knows nothing. She resolved to keep out of his way, not to meet his eyes, perhaps pretend not to recognise him. They were bound to bump into each other in the next few days, but she would play it safe.

A slim woman with an air of impenetrable calm settled on the sofa beside her. She wore a long tie-and-dye skirt and a Navajo blanket cape. An 'Om' symbol was tattooed on her wrist. Her eyes were closed and she was breathing slowly. Although she was clearly an American, she had folded her legs in Padmasana and sat straight and still in perfect yogic posture.

The women opened her eyes and smiled. She had a lined face and the most youthful eyes Gayatri had ever encountered. 'Sorry to be doing this here,' she said. 'I was just trying to centre myself. This festival, much as I love it, is an assault on the senses. I'm plain overstimulated.

'I'm returning to India after a very long time,' she continued. 'Eternal India. It's changed and yet it hasn't. Like everything else, I suppose. I'm Anna Wilde, and I'm here with my new book of meditation practice. It's called *The Third Way*. It's an old book, really, but it's been reissued - sort of reborn, I suppose. That and my travelogue, *The Inner Eye*, which I wrote before that.'

Gayatri turned suddenly effusive. Anna Wilde. The name struck a chord. She knew of the books, she had heard of Anna Wilde and the woman's association with the Beat Poets, with Allen Ginsberg. She dimly remembered reading *The Inner Eye* in college.

'Delighted to meet you ...absolutely honoured! I'm Gayatri - Gayatri Smyth Gandhy. I'm an anthropologist.'

From the corner of her eye, Gayatri could glimpse Sumedh leave the room. His wife didn't follow him but remained in the authors' lounge, searching for something in her festival cloth bag, before wandering off via the other exit.

'I teach Theology at the University of Colorado,' Anna said, in chaste Hindi. 'I suppose you could call me a Hindu, by dharma and by karma. I lived in Kashi for six years, in Benares, by the banks of the Ganga, studying the scriptures and learning from my guru. Then I awoke from my dream, and returned to my own land.'

Gayatri found herself telling Anna about her novel, about the complex theme, invoking Yama, the Lord of Death, and Kama, the God of Love. She had never told anyone of this, and she was surprised by her confession.

Anna Wilde nodded sagely, as though she perfectly understood the plot and its connotations. 'I'm glad someone is paying their respects to Lord Yama,' she observed gravely. 'Far too many in the world have forgotten that he exists, are unaware that he rules our lives. As for me, I have lived in his arms, in his service, with my Aghora guru - my then Guru - amidst the ashes of the burning ghats of Kashi.'

Two things happened as she made this startling declaration. A pigeon fluttered down from the balcony above and splattered a mass of grey excreta on Gayatri's arm. At almost precisely the same moment, Sumedh Kumar re-entered the room and fell into a dead faint.

Gayatri could have run towards the washroom to wipe the mess off her arms, but instead she rushed to where Sumedh Kumar was lying inert on the floor.

A volunteer had arrived, with a man who appeared to be a doctor. Together, they carried him into an anteroom which had a couch and a four-poster bed. The volunteer, a thin boy with pimples, sprinkled water on his face while the doctor felt his pulse.

Sumedh Kumar's eyes fluttered open. He looked around him, at the four-poster bed (which he noticed was carved with an intricate pattern of entwined pineapples), at the doctor, at the alarmed volunteer, and at her. He looked puzzled, then pleased.

'*Arre*, Gayatri! What are you doing here?' he enquired, sounding surprised and reassured in equal measure.

In that moment, she stopped being who she was, and returned to the person she had once been. She wiped off the pigeon shit with some tissues the helpful young man had proffered, and went to the washroom to soap off the remains. It was as though her metabolism, the very flow of her blood, had been renewed, the debris of regrets and rejection washed away by those few words. She fixed her lipstick and patted her hair into place.

His auburn-haired wife returned around then. She seemed flustered but not surprised. 'It's happened before,' she explained to the doctor. 'I have his prescription and medical record on my phone. Give me your number and I'll WhatsApp it to you ...

'He seems fine now,' she concluded, after she had sent the details across. 'Aren't you fine now, darling?' she asked Sumedh, baring her teeth into a smile.

'Yes, I'm fine now, Carmen,' Sumedh Kumar replied levelly.

Gayatri was struck by the colour of his wife's teeth, how large they were, and how yellow. She tried not to think about the woman's teeth, pretend to herself that she had not noticed them.

Carmen then left the room and returned in no time with the medical records. 'Thank God we are staying close to the festival premises!' she exclaimed. 'Right - Pico Iyer is speaking in the Front Lawn, and Angela has saved a seat for me ...' With these words she hurried away, leaving an air of literary urgency in her wake.

The doctor was studying the medical file Carmen Kumar had handed him. 'Hmm,' he said, then 'Hmm,' again, more thoughtfully this time. He turned to Gayatri as though she was the woman in charge.

'I wouldn't be comfortable just letting him be,' the doctor informed her. 'He should be under observation, in the Festival hospital. It's just around the corner, and we have reserved some rooms for delegates.'

A wheelchair was produced, and the doctor, Sumedh Kumar, Gayatri Smyth Gandhy and the young volunteer, whose name they had discovered was Vikrant, set out against the tide, jostling through the milling crowds who were coming to hear a Bollywood Bad Boy who had just written an indiscreet tell-all.

They were transported in an ambulance, which smelt inexplicably of jasmine and roses, to a hospital which was, as the doctor had promised, just around the corner. It was a cool calm place illumined by blue fluorescent lights, which made everything look as though it were being X-rayed.

Sumedh Kumar stroked Gayatri's arm, gently, meditatively. The hair on his knuckles was grey. Gayatri's arms had been waxed just a fortnight ago, but there was a crop of sharp new stubble that rose to meet his touch.

The observation room, #1088, was lit up with the same dim blue lighting, except for a single beam of yellow emanating from a steel bedside lamp.

Having been deposited in the observation room, and the patient settled into the bed there, they were then left to themselves except for a visit from a busy nurse who took Sumedh's temperature and fussed around with the drip that hung by the hospital bed. She asked him concernedly how he was feeling, and draped an enormous towel around his neck. A meal tray arrived, with a mess of sambhar, boiled vegetables and custard.

Gayatri and Sumedh looked at each other in the blue light broken by the yellow beam. He seemed amused by the situation, and winked at her conspiratorially every now and then. He dozed off for a while, and she looked at him, a well of familiar tenderness opening out inside her.

He awoke with a start. 'I'd better tell Carmen I'm here,' he said, and sent off a text message to apprise his wife of his whereabouts.

They looked at each other, and smiled. Her linear mind, with its understanding of sequential dates and consequential actions, seemed to have shut down. This was the present, but it was also the past. There was an inevitability to their meeting like this, under such unexpected circumstances.

'Let's get out of here,' he whispered. There was a manic look in his eyes. 'I can't take this blue light any more. It's driving me crazy.'

He guided her out, in the gentlemanly way she remembered so well, and led her down from the Fire Exit. 'Not the lifts,' he said, 'or they won't let us leave.'

Room #1088 seemed inexplicably to have been on the third floor. They lurched out into the lobby, where a man in a striped Rajasthani turban was being wheeled in. His face was ashen and still, and the white sheet draped over him had stains of blood on it. It was the balladeer Mohan Bhopa, and his wife the Bhopi. What had happened to him? The balladeer didn't recognise her; didn't register that Gayatri had introduced him on the stage just yesterday.

But his wife did. The Bhopi was weeping as she followed the Bhopa on his stretcher. She held out her hands imploringly and said something in Rajasthani to Gayatri.

This was not the moment, this was not the place. Gayatri pulled her cashmere scarf around her face and pretended not to have seen them.

Sumedh Kumar didn't let her stop. He steered her out into the porch, and then they were on the main road, where the traffic whooshed around them like an angry battalion of night animals, an advancing army of darkness.

'Let's go to your hotel,' he murmured. Then he kissed her ear; his tongue scooped into its crevices, left a ring of spit around her diamond earrings. She was shocked but also delighted. Some things were preordained, were meant to be.

They settled into an auto-rickshaw and arrived outside the arched gates of the Padmini Nivas Hotel. She felt very close to him, in the dusty dark, amidst the noise of the traffic.

She collected her key from the reception while he waited in the garden, and they entered her room together with the furtive secrecy of old-fashioned lovers.

He drank a glass of water from the plastic bottles that stood lined up on the dresser, before lying down on her bed and shutting his eyes. She sat on an ornate teak chair, contemplating him. His eyes were shut, but he was smiling. It was a smile she knew, and remembered, with the laugh lines - many more of them now than then - bracketing his lips. Outside, the harsh cry of a peacock, and an owl hooting, though it was surely too early in the night for owls to be hooting. What was the time?

Then she lay down beside him, their bodies fitting into each other quite naturally, as they had done before.

He fell asleep but she did not. She stayed awake most of the night, listening to him breathe. When dawn broke, and a crick of light showed through the carelessly drawn curtains, he kissed her, gently and slowly, and went back to sleep again.

She fell asleep at last and dreamed of the balladeer, the Bhopa, and his songs. When she awoke, Sumedh was gone. He had not woken her, but slipped out again from her life as he had done all those years ago, returned to a woman with large yellow teeth.

Gayatri lingered over her morning coffee. The peacocks were calling outside. The sky was a brilliant blue. Perhaps it had all been a dream, a dream with an edge of nightmare. She needed time to herself to process this, to come to terms with it, to wonder what it might lead to.

Just then, she received a call on her landline from the festival. The programme director was on the line.

The Bhopa had died. He had been hit by an auto-rickshaw while crossing the road, and was taken to the hospital, where he succumbed to internal wounds.

They were organising a special tribute to him, the programme director informed her, to be slotted into place during the morning music. They would play a video clip from his performance, which had been just two days ago, when Gayatri Smyth Gandhy had been in conversation with him. The audience would be asked to observe two minutes of silence in his memory.

Would she read a tribute to the balladeer? Just a few words, in memoriam?

Gayatri was consumed by guilt. She had been there, at the hospital, when they wheeled him in. His wife had reached out to her, but Gayatri had stepped back, covered her head with her shawl, pretended not to have seen her.

'Let me think about it,' she said. 'I seem to be running a high temperature today. I will turn up if I'm feeling any better.'

There was a special hell reserved for people like her. She could have responded to that plea for help, turned back to see if she was needed. Repentance and remorse were of no use now, though; they could not correct that misconduct.

In her mind's eye, she was a young girl again, living here in Jaipur with her parents. It was a sweltering summer day. Her friend had come to spend the afternoon with her. They were looking for an indoor space in which to play ball. She had reached out to remove an old scroll that hung on the wall. It depicted a turbaned hero riding a saffron-hued horse, a procession of veiled women, a herd of demure cows, a tiger, a camel and an unlikely-looking bird.

Something had gone wrong with the ball, the scroll, a table and a vase of flowers. There was a loud crash and splintered glass, water, flowers all over the floor. The chowkidar had heard the crash and come in to check what was happening. He had bent down reverentially to pick up the scroll, and placed it on a high table out of their reach.

The chowkidar wore a turban and had a fierce moustache. He had bent down on his knees and spoken gently to them. 'Baisa, sister, you don't do this. Pabuji is god and the Phad is his temple. You bring bad luck if respect is not shown.'

The memory of that afternoon had been completely obliterated for decades now. It rose within her as though it had happened yesterday - that guilt, that sense of violation of a sacred space.

No, she couldn't go on stage and read out a tribute. Not after her disgraceful behaviour. And what if his wife, the Bhopi, was there? How could she ever face her again?

The Bhopa's death was mentioned in the local newspapers, in the *Rajasthan Patrika*, and the *Hindustan Times* as well. 'The End of a Legacy,' the headline said. He was to be cremated in his village, near Bikaner.

The wife would have returned to the village too. Perhaps it *was* her duty to go on stage, Gayatri thought, to make amends, to speak for him and the Bhopi, and the sacred scroll that she remembered from her childhood.

She composed herself and settled down with her laptop to work on the tribute. There was so much to say, so little time to say it.

'Madan Bhopa was the last in a legacy of storytellers and healers devoted to Pabuji. His departure from this world is like a metaphor for the death of the fantastical oral traditions he stood for. Although he is described on the internet as an "illiterate goatherd", his education began at the age of four, when his father began teaching him to memorise the epic. He soon learnt to hold the equivalent of 600 pages of text in his head. The Phad scroll is a portable shrine, to illustrate the narrative of the folk hero Pabuji. The story originated in the villages around Bikaner in the fourteenth century, to a community of nomadic pastoralists. Their god and his temple travelled easily with them as a rolled-up scroll. When the sun dipped over the desert horizon and the families set up their tents, on special nights, the Bhopa, the traditional storyteller, and his wife would spread out the scroll as a backdrop for communal worship, and they would narrate the epic of Pabuji. Madan Bhopa was an accomplished and versatile artist and storyteller. His wife, Misra Devi, was herself the daughter of a bard. She was trained as a Phad narrator by her husband and parents-in-law. I salute them both, and the heroic traditions of Rajasthan, where I had the good fortune to live for some years as a child.' That was enough, she decided; she did not need to say any more. And anyway, words were inadequate to describe the sense of inconsolable loss she felt.

She made her way to the festival and read out the tribute she had written. There were many locals from Jaipur, and from around Rajasthan, in the audience, and she sensed that they could scan the distance between the precise English words she employed and the collective loss they felt. The others were moved too, she could see that they were, but the distances between their lives were too deep for them to possibly comprehend or understand what the Bhopa stood for and represented.

Gayatri returned to the hotel after that. She decided to skip the overcrowded panel discussion she was scheduled to speak at in the afternoon, and made her excuses on that front. She sent another email from her room. 'I am running a high temperature' (the standard excuse of her Indian student days). 'I have seen a doctor and he has advised complete bedrest. Will let you know how I am doing. Thank you for your understanding.'

She began again on her novel that afternoon, archiving rather than deleting the opening she had previously worked on. It now featured a woman who meets her old lover and discovers he is terminally ill. He tells her he loves her still. It sounded much too sentimental, and she put it away resignedly. 'Maybe I'm just not cut out to be a novelist,' she told herself, 'and life is so much stranger than fiction anyway.'

Somebody had slipped a letter under the door. She picked it up, curious. Perhaps Sumedh had sent her a love letter, or apologised for his stealthy departure.

It was addressed to her, in a sloping italic hand. It had a glossy picture of a kitten playing with a ball of purple wool. Inside, the same handwriting, in purple ink.

'You BICH,' it said. 'You posturing plagiarist. This is culchural condescension and all-too-typical colonial-style appropriation. Do you even realise that you live off the folk artistes and musicians you talk so glibly about? I wonder what they have to say about *you*. You may think you are so WOKE, but you have no skin in the game!'

It was not signed. She had no clue who could have slipped it under the door. It would have shocked her on any other day, but today it devastated her. She lay on the sofa and wept, for herself, for so many things remembered and forgotten and that might have been.

Rudrani Rana was in her room, eating a Subway sandwich, pondering the day. She had particularly enjoyed the session on ghazals and Urdu poetry. She was snobbish about Hindi writers but Urdu was Urdu and Javed Akhtar was, when all was said and done, a very erudite man. What was the phrase about time in the poem he had read? 'Time is like a bird that keeps flying.'

'No,' she told herself, 'time is like a train that halts and proceeds, and sometimes gets derailed.'

Rudrani had taken the train from Nizamuddin East to Jaipur Junction. She would take the same train back when the festival wound to a close. The homestay she had booked was frugal but comfortable. The two sisters who let out their spare bedroom looked at her with respect, and addressed her as Professor Sahiba. She liked that.

She had ambiguous feelings about trains. She loved them but they carried an underbelly of anxiety and dread. She had never forgotten the Dehradun Express, and that first visit to Delhi when she was eleven. The terrors of the toilet, of that dark swaying hole in the dank train floor that threatened to pull her in, to engulf and obliterate her. The fear of it consumed her, like the other unspoken terrors she faced.

The train from Dehradun passed through an interminably long tunnel. On that first journey, when she was eleven, she had encountered stark terror as she felt herself being swallowed up by the dark. She had tried to hold on to her mother, but that wasn't enough, it never had been.

She had clung on fearfully to her mother's hand - but Mummy pinched her, impatiently, dismissively - and the pain of her strong hard fingers banished the terror of the darkness outside.

The excitement of the successive railway stations took over, the tea vendors, the red-shirted coolies, the blurred images of families assembled on the platforms, waving as the train steamed off, with the whistle blowing in her ears like a bugle. And so she got over her fear of the dark tunnels, but not completely, not for ever.

Rudrani enjoyed the literature festival as she had enjoyed those train journeys: people everywhere, and she herself alone and yet not alone amidst those milling crowds.

She could still remember with cold clarity the first time she had written a letter - *that* sort of a letter. What she called a truth letter. It was to the wife of the man who had troubled her, who continued to trouble her, and who had troubled her mother as well. The bad man who the world thought was such a good man, who stood tall at assembly, telling everyone what they should do and not do, as though he knew better than the schoolchildren who stood in neat lines before him, in the windy quadrangle, waiting for classes to begin.

'Dear Madam, you think your esteemed husband is a good man? No, the old so-and-so is a BASTARD and he troubles and torments poor innocent souls. Please tell him about this letter and STOP him. Otherwise, every teacher in school will get this LETTER.'

And she did send the truth letters to all the teachers, even though she was afraid some of them might recognise her handwriting. She tried to slope the italics the other way to confuse them, and put in lots of capital letters as a sort of disguise. Yet somewhere she didn't care if they knew it was her; in fact, she almost wished they would find out.

'This LETTER is to tell you how you are being FOOLED by that BASTARD who you think is a good upright man.

He has bad BREATH and his SOUL also stinks. This school should EXPEL him. Please SPIT on him the NEXT time you see him, though all the SPIT in the WORLD cannot cleanse him of his VILE acts and his SINS. PLEASE STOP him.'

Nobody took any notice of her letters, but still it helped her to write them, and to send them. She had once spat on him during school assembly, and after that her mother decided to move to Delhi and they left Dehradun for ever. In Karol Bagh, the central district of Delhi, the girl missed the joys of Rajpur Road, and the city of Ghaziabad, east of Delhi, was not much better.

After the move, Rudrani Rana continued to work on her truth letters. It was a hobby, a craft, a project. She was objective and just: she spared no one. Except Stella Murch. She had torn up that letter after she wrote it, and never penned another one.

Zoya Mankotia had been inordinately affected by the anonymous letter. She was accustomed to being reviled and abused by patriarchal trolls, and she could give as well as she got on ideology. But she had no idea why a purple envelope with a sentimental pretty kitty card should open up to call her a 'BICH'.

Who could have written it? Who had penned the message in that sloping italic hand? Why did he or she hate her so much? And how did they know she was cheating on her wife?

Zoya Mankotia was working on a book on sorority and women's movements. It troubled her to think that the anonymous note could have come, as Shonali Sen had suggested, from another woman. Not that it would be any more heartening to learn that the poison pen belonged to a man, or a transgender, or someone of any colour of rainbow identity.

Zoya was introduced to Anirban M. by a mutual friend. 'He is working on a series titled *Faces of the Festival*,' she was told in an effusive email connecting her to the graphic crossover artist.

Anirban studied Zoya Mankotia's attractive, unusual face, and was charmed by it. Her flowing grey hair had the texture of liquid stone, a volcanic stone perhaps, or granite, or jasper. Jasper, he decided, as he studied her animated face, her swift movements.

'I'm so very agitated,' she sighed, as they got to chatting. 'There is so much hatred in our world, so much harm. It's difficult to believe we are all humans on this planet - it seems to get more dystopian every day.'

Anirban listened to her, distractedly. He was composing a picture, sketching her in his mind.

Zoya Mankotia handed him the purple envelope. 'I got this, yesterday,' she said, wiping a tear from the corner of her eye. 'I don't know what to do about it. It's hit me somewhere. I can't seem to get over it.'

He was still wondering about how he would portray her hair. Smudged charcoal, he thought.

Just then, the Bollywood star Patti Kapoor walked into the lounge with a crowd of fans in her wake, all struggling to break through the barriers even as the volunteers tried to keep them at bay. There was a charge around the woman that was visible, tangible and electric.

'Look at that,' Zoya said bitterly. 'These so-called literary festivals! This bimbo hasn't written a word, or even read one, I'm sure.'

Anirban was struck by the venom in her voice. 'I always thought you women stuck together?' he said gently. 'Patti Kapoor is a really fine actress. Cinema and the moving image provide another form of narrative. The performative arts are as important as textuality ...'

But he had lost her attention. She had flounced off to another session.

It was only when he was back in his room, in the cheerful modern hotel where he had been accommodated, that the coincidence struck him. He was considering the sketch he had made the day before. It was of an older woman with a mass of untidy white hair held up in a loose bun, and a face that must once have been strikingly beautiful. She looked like Virginia Woolf.

What was her name? He struggled to remember. Rudrani Rana, that was it. She had told him: 'I'm a failed novelist. I write anonymous letters. To signal to the world what I am thinking. To let them know.'

It all came back to him. The troglodyte. She must have sent Zoya Mankotia that strange, malicious card.

An unexpected flicker of affection rose within him. Once again, she reminded him of his widowed aunt, his Mashi-ma. She was a fighter, he recognised that, and it was the fight that kept her going. He would keep her secret, he surely would, and he would seek her again amidst the milling throngs of book-lovers and writers and all those around who were searching for their own, or any, story.

A passing comment at a session he had attended that afternoon had lodged itself in his memory. 'Anonymity is the greatest spur to creativity,' a bespectacled writer from Kerala had observed, 'for to be nameless confers the power to be protean.'

The words had struck a chord in him. They described the joy he felt floating through the festival, navigating his way through the crowds, unnoticed and unobserved, even as his keen eyes noticed and registered every nuance of posture and expression. He felt he was a camera, zooming in, zooming out, moving from burst mode to blurred backgrounds, before his lens settled on the most inessential image which was in truth the heart of the visual narrative.

Anirban's secret project, his column *Eye Spye*, gave him a delicious double life as he listened in to the public and private conversations of the speakers and audiences. He savoured the mantle of invisibility that came with being one with the mass, of blending into the background.

As a child, he had often dreamed of becoming invisible, of seeing and knowing everything without being seen or known. The *Eye Spye* column helped him live out that fantasy, allowed him to become an agile shapeshifter with the power to observe the personalities he encountered and to pin them to paper with his sharp and acute sketches.

Patti Kapoor was to launch Ketan's new book, and the weekend crush was building up into a relentless deluge. Anirban M. found himself whistling as he sidestepped wheelchairs, hordes of selfie-seekers, armies of schoolchildren, and hapless international tourists bewildered and bemused by being in one of the most crowded spots on Planet Earth.

He was whistling the tune from a Beatles song, as he often did. It was not 'Ob-La-Di, Ob-La Da' today; as the whistling turned to a hum, he took note of the words he was singing, under his breath, like a mantra. They came from 'Eleanor Rigby'. And as this dawned on him, he discovered that he was watching out for the figure of an elderly lady. That's who she was, of course. The original Eleanor Rigby.

But he didn't see her anywhere, not at the Front Lawn, nor at the slam poetry or at the charged sessions on the ahistorical understanding of India's past. Where would she be? he wondered. At the Sanskrit session? The panel on environmental justice? He thought he glimpsed her at the Durbar Hall, emerging from a dialogue between a Bangla Dalit poet and her Latvian translator. The trailing sari, the two bags ...but she was gone before he could reach her.

Rudrani Rana sat in her modest room, struggling to remove her facial hair. She could have gone to a beauty parlour but she was fastidious; the cheap ones were dirty, the upmarket ones unaffordable.

It was like a surgical operation. She placed her enlarging mirror on the bed and sat down on a stool beside it, holding a torch to her chin. Up close, her face looked frightening. The magnified pores, the whorls of flesh on her sagging chin, the hairy nostrils, the spikes of white that bristled in the most unexpected spots: the afflictions of age, which she accepted, which she battled.

She set to work on removing the hairs, wielding the rusting tweezers patiently, methodically, and with laser precision. She hummed to herself, even as she winced at that final moment when she plucked out the stubborn roots. Led Zeppelin, 1971. She was in her twenties again, and had just returned to Dehradun for some reason she couldn't now recall. Rajpur Road, with the smells of frying samosa and jalebis, and posters of Zeenat Aman on the walls and billboards. Dev Anand had just released the movie *Hare Rama Hare Krishna* and its most popular song 'Dum Maro Dum' was playing everywhere. She had stepped into Kwality to buy herself some of the famous fudge, and it was there that she first heard them, Jimmy Page and Robert Plant, singing as though just for her.

The opening riff, and then the mystical words of 'Stairway to Heaven'.

She sat there, then, at Kwality's in Rajpur Road, mouthing the words. She had ordered a milkshake, and asked them to play the song again. The boy at the counter turned the stylus back and the LP record began revolving at 33 1/3 rpm.

And here she was, in her seventies, with just that same teetering see-saw of hope and despair she had felt then. Plucking at the hairs on her time-ravaged face.

'The Answer Lies in the Whispering Wind' was the title of the first short story she had ever attempted, based loosely on the lyrics of the song. Neatly handwritten, in sloping italics, in a lined notebook. Six versions, with each set of corrections carried forward until she was satisfied, or almost satisfied.

Rudrani had joined a stenography course after that, subsidised by Stella Murch's munificence.

Afterwards, she had moved back to Dehradun, seeking the outlines of the nearby foothills already waiting to greet her in Rajpur. She had returned for the evening breeze, for the memories of her mother, for her lost childhood.

It was exhilarating to learn how to type. The enigma of the QWERTY keyboard, with its Back Space, Shift Key, Caps Lock. Her long fingers with their perfectly shaped scarlet nails going furiously for the keys. Clackety Clack. Clackety Clack. She had memorised the keyboard until she felt it was imprinted in her mind's eye. 'Touch and tap, not hunt and peck,' she would tell herself, admiring her nails as they hit the keys with the most delightful precision.

The Quick Brown Fox Jumps Over The Lazy Dog. That was how she had begun another of her short stories, fascinated by how this one cryptic sentence encapsulated all the letters of the alphabet.

Many of those early experiments were about words, and feelings, and how the two translated into each other. These stories were mostly despairing, though in her own private critiques she would think of them as 'wry', or 'ironic'.

Until she met Rupert Murch. His mother, the formidable Stella Murch, had been her mother's friend. The relationship between the two women had been complicated, with several layers of rivalry, suspicion and Schadenfreude puncturing the surface cordiality.

Rudrani Rana's father, Parashuram Prajapati Rana (PP to his friends), was descended from a rich Nepalese family. They had lost their lands and fortune, the mango orchards and rice fields around Dehradun and the vast land grants they had received from the Gurkhali dispensation in the days of the expanding Gurkha empire. There were just seven acres left, which were under bitter litigation.

Her mother, Tara, was a local Bisht girl; their family had converted to Christianity, and Tara had a Scottish grandmother who she constantly invoked.

Rudrani had only hazy memories of her father. Apparently he had been charming and learned and fond of shooting and hunting. He had put a revolver to his forehead on Rudrani's first birthday. There had been a police inquiry and a post mortem. It had been declared a case of suicide.

Rudrani's mother never spoke of the past. It was as though it did not exist, as if her daughter had been born of her mother and her mother alone. Rudrani kept to the contract and never asked about her father. She knew the details of his death, if not his life, from the newspaper cutting glued to a large black photo album kept in a trunk under her mother's bed.

Stella Murch was a senior teacher in the school where Mrs Rana was the matron. She was an Anglo-Indian from an established railway family. Like Mrs Rana, she too was a widow. She had a son - the incredibly handsome Rupert Murch.

Rudrani awoke from the sea of dreaming memories to re-examine the reflection of her face. The folding contraption with the magnifying mirror had a distortion around the edges. It made her look like an extinct sea animal, struggling to tweeze out its delicate whiskers. Her grey eyes had specks of pale blue in them.

'Your eyes ...you get them from my Scottish grandmother,' her mother would tell her, as she combed Rudrani's hair into neat double plaits. Those eyes were now set in radial wrinkles, like an unfolding Japanese fan. Her mother's Scottish grandmother's eyes.

She made an affectionate moue at her reflection. 'Sonnet 64,' she said, in Stella Murch's Anglo-Indian English teacher's voice. 'Open your books at Sonnet 64.'

When I have seen by Time's fell hand defac'd/The rich proud cost of outworn buried age.

Mrs Murch had struggled valiantly to teach her class Shakespeare. She found the language incomprehensible, the references obscure, and puzzled over much of what she was teaching. She didn't really have a feel for literature, but had been assigned the subject out of respect for her English ancestry.

Mrs Murch would resort to a 'subject guide' purchased from the local bookshop, which she kept covered in a brown paper cover. It was called *Shakespeare Sonnets* by Ram Lalla. Young Rudrani had smirked to herself when she observed the teacher's unheroic struggles with the Bard. 'This sonnet is discussing how Time destroys everything eventually. One day, all of you young ladies will grow old, and you will understand the meaning of this poem.'

Rudrani had raised her hand. 'Mrs Murch, what is the exact difference between a poem and a sonnet?' she had asked. 'And what exactly is a quatrain?'

She knew the answer, but wanted to trip the teacher up. Expose her.

The woman was, predictably, flustered. 'We are discussing the theme, not the structure, my dear,' she replied. 'But since you have asked, perhaps you could write an essay on the subject and submit it next Thursday?'

'Of course, Mrs Murch,' she replied obediently. She had spent the weekend in the Parade Ground library searching for any snatches of information. She couldn't remember now what she had written in that carefully worded essay, but she could still recall her exhilaration in reading Shakespeare not as a chore but as a challenge.

On the coming Thursday, Rudrani had duly presented the essay to Mrs Murch. 'May I read it out in class?' she had asked.

'I am the teacher, not you. Why on earth would I ask *you* to read it out to the class, Rudrani?' Stella Murch had replied. She had lifted one eyebrow and put on a sarcastic expression that made her look as though she had suffered a facial stroke.

Mrs Murch had never bothered to correct or grade the essay; when Rudrani asked her if she had read it, she had simply replied: 'It's under a pile of papers somewhere. I will read it someday.'

Yet it was the same Mrs Murch who had offered to pay for her stenography course, funded by a trust that had requested the teacher to find five suitable women candidates for skill training. Two nurses, two teachers and a stenographer.

Perhaps the woman had been fond of her, in her own way, despite the essay on Shakespeare's Sonnet 64.

Perhaps she had also forgiven Mrs Rana for the fraught conversations and minor rivalries that had defined their friendship.

When Rudrani met Rupert Murch, when she had fallen in love with him, she thought that perhaps his mother might consider her, Rudrani, as a future daughter-in-law.

They met over a game of ping-pong in the YMCA, and then at a jam session at a new restaurant opposite Kwality's. Rupert Murch was the handsomest young man Rudrani Rana had ever met. He was also friendly, and kind, comfortable to be with.

She had written a short story the week after she met him. It was a romantic tale, optimistic and full of hope. The *Pioneer* accepted her offering for their weekend session. It was the only story she wrote that was ever published. Rudrani still remembered how it had begun.

I was a young woman viewing the world with fascination, writing stories from my overflowing heart. Those were the opening words. It had been a love story, about a woman writing a love story.

How naive she had been, how silly. That story was over, the narrative lost in old newsprint, with no trace of it remaining.

She thought of the novel sitting stoically in its canvas bag, indifferent to its fate, content in the act of being written, in its own proud existence. The book remained unsubmitted, impervious to readers and opinions. Sometimes she even forgot its working title, *The Face by the Window*. *UNSUBMITTED* was more appropriate. The magnum opus was one of a kind, rejecting clichés, resisting platitudes, defying linear narrative to create a mosaic in which the true pattern showed up only to the eye that could follow it.

She put away the mirror, and the torch, and the tweezers, and sat down to finish the Subway sandwich she had bought herself on the way home.

Time for bed. It was a busy day tomorrow. She wanted to be there for the very first session, after the morning music. Five writers from five continents on 'Why I Write'. She had marked the other sessions on her programme too. Perhaps she would meet the young man again, the one who had called himself an outsider. Anirban, Anirban M. - was that his name?

Raju Srivastava sat in the dark, shadowy bar, drinking Indian whisky, absentmindedly chewing at a bowl of peanuts. The brown skin of the nuts lay scattered before him, like insect wings. In the garden outside, a woman was singing a ghazal in a shrill voice. She had got the cadence of the verses wrong, but it was still a pleasing distraction.

The whisky and the music and the exhilaration of encountering Javed Akhtar had built up to a fulfilled buzz inside him. He felt on the threshold, of the past, and the future. It was as though he had climbed the peak of a storybook mountain: he could see the vista of his future spread out before him. The epochal poet 'Betaab', speaking for his times.

He fumbled in his smart leather man-pouch for his book, that slender volume of poetry which he planned to leave for Janab Javed Akhtar in his room the next day. *The Thief of Time* by Razi Khan Singh 'Betaab'. Although his nom de plume of 'Betaab' remained the same, he had decided to adopt another identity for his formal outing as a poet. His birth name, Raju Srivastava, did not carry the necessary resonance. It reminded the young man that even with the imposing adoption of 'Betaab', he was still the son of a failed tailor. To make matters worse, there was another Raju Srivastava, a popular, almost legendary stand-up comedian, with a squeaky voice and a silly style of jokes. The self-born Razi Khan Singh 'Betaab' could be what and who he wanted, straddling cultures and identities with élan and impunity.

Raju imagined Razi Khan Singh to be the Rajput son of a highborn lady of Lucknow, the child of a star-crossed love affair. Nobility and honour flowed in his veins, and his every breath was poetry, the impatient fire within contained - if it could be contained - in the words of Betaab.

The book was titled *Waqt Chor*. *The Thief of Time*. It could also, he supposed, translate into *Time the Thief*. The title of the book was embossed on the cover in delicate silver, in elegant Urdu calligraphy as well as the more stolid Devanagari script. Inside, a hundred poems, a torrent of fury and regret, longing and hope.

*

The story of Betaab's birth as a poet began with demonetisation, and the stacks of 1000-rupee notes he had put away after a well-executed burglary.

It was 8 November 2016. There was a chill in the air outside, as was to be expected after Diwali. Pollution levels had spiked, as they always did at this time of the year. Raju Srivastava had been idly switching channels on the TV when he chanced upon the announcement that forever changed his life.

Prime Minister Narendra Modi appeared on the screen, searching the eyes of every Indian hooked to prime-time news. He was dressed in a natty cream Jawahar jacket. The flag of India hung limply behind him. The podium he spoke from had the three lions of the Ashoka emblem etched in shining gold. They represented Satyameva Jayate: the national motto of India, meaning Truth Will Prevail.

Modi-ji was preparing to make a key announcement. He looked grave yet somehow breathless with excitement. 'My dear fellow citizens, I hope you ended the festive season of Diwali with joy and new hope. Today I will be speaking to you about some critical issues and important decisions.'

Raju's mobile phone was ringing but he couldn't find it to switch off. In the midst of this confusion he heard fragments of Modi's speech. *The* speech.

'Sisters and brothers …To rid the nation of the termites of black money and corruption …' and then his mobile phone rang again, from a number he did not recognise, drowning out the prime minister's voice.

Raju switched his phone off, and heard: 'From midnight tonight, the eighth of November 2016, 500-rupee and 1000-rupee currency notes will no longer be legal tender.'

It took some time for the words to sink in. What was the prime minister saying? What sort of joke was this?

Modi-ji spoke on in his theatrical, seductive voice. His eyes reaching out to Raju Srivastava, to a billion and a quarter Indians. 'To break the grip of corruption …'

Money was the king, the ruler, the bulwark of lives. Had Modi-ji gone mad? Was Raju Srivastava 'Betaab' dreaming? Was this a practical joke? Or some sort of monstrous hallucination?

He switched channels to see what they were saying.

'The 500-rupee and 1000-rupee currency notes presently in use will no longer be legal tender from midnight tonight, that is, from eighth November 2016. This means these notes will not be acceptable for transactions from midnight onwards. The notes hoarded by anti-national and antisocial elements will become just worthless pieces of paper. The rights of honest, hardworking people will continue to be fully protected. Let me assure you that notes of one hundred, fifty, twenty, ten, five, two and one rupee and all coins will remain legal tender and will not be affected.'

Raju had poured himself a glass of cold water from the fridge. He drank it down in one long gulp, then sat down before the television screen and began laughing. He roared out loud, and then the howls and shrieks of helpless laughter subsided into squeals and yelps of pain, to convulsions of the stomach, until tears clotted his vision.

He went to the steel cupboard that doubled as a bar and took out a bottle of Johnnie Walker Double Black whisky. Prime Minister Modi was still saying the same things again and again.

'After midnight, 500-rupee and 1000-rupee currency notes will no longer be legal tender.' 'Sisters and brothers ...' 'Honest, hardworking citizens will not be affected.' Raju fortified the whisky with ice cubes and took a very large mouthful. Then he knelt down before the small shrine to Lakshmi, the Goddess of Wealth, situated on the bottom shelf of the same steel Godrej cupboard that doubled as a bar.

'Mother!' he pleaded. 'Ma Lakshmi! You may think I am not honest, but you know I am hardworking. And I have never disrespected you. So what do I do now? Guide me, Mother Lakshmi.'

Leaving that rhetorical plea hanging in the air, he walked into the bathroom in his compact one-bedroom flat. The bathing area had been boarded up to create a wall-to-wall cupboard covered with mirrored glass. This opened into a shelved cupboard, secured with iron grills. There were ten suitcases inside this hidden cupboard, all of different sizes. Raju took out one of the smaller ones, a cabin-sized stroller, and locked the cupboard again. He finished the Double Black whisky in a few quick gulps, then set off for Pushpa Shopping Mall in Noida.

Raju Srivastava didn't like to draw attention to himself. He lived modestly in a decent neighbourhood in Noida.

No servants. No driver. The place had no nameplate and he tipped the security guards, but not too generously, for their goodwill.

He drove himself to Pushpa Mall. Even at this late hour, it was awash with lights and aflutter with activity. The jewellery segment on the third floor had a crowd of agitated customers who were, quite literally, buying up all they could lay their hands on. He could hear the rustle of notes, the chatter of frenzied voices. The clatter of gold chains, gold necklaces, gold bangles, gold ear-tops, dangling gold *jhumkas*.

He wasn't the only one to have come with a suitcase. People were carrying bags, jholas, even baskets of money. The shopkeeper had a glazed look in his eyes as he counted the piled-up wads of notes fortressed around him. Raju found it impossible to get his attention. He waited patiently for a while, then leant over and tapped the man on the shoulder. The shopkeeper still didn't respond, and so 'Betaab' began shaking and nudging at his shoulder impatiently.

'Yes, yes, brother, I am coming to help you,' the shopkeeper said distractedly. An old woman in a crumpled sari and white hair tied into a severe knot came and stood herself before Raju.

'I am his mother,' she said. 'I will attend to you.'

Something about her reminded Raju of his own mother, and he bent down to touch her wrinkled feet, shod in ancient rubber chappals, worn at the heels. Her toenails had traces of faded red polish.

'Help me, Mother,' he said emotionally. 'Think of me as your son.'

'We have run out of gold,' she replied, 'but I shall try to help you.' She led him behind the sales desk to a small cabin the size of a cupboard.

After fiddling for some time with the numerical lock, the old woman extracted a pile of gold chains and bangles. She placed them on the weighing scales and then took out a battered calculator. Raju observed her patiently, grateful for her attention.

'Two chains, fourteen bangles,' she muttered. 'That's all I have left. Sixteen lakhs for the lot.'

Raju knew she was overcharging him, cheating him. 'I don't have a wife, or even a sister,' he protested. 'What will I do with gold bangles, Mother?'

'Why - wear them!' she taunted, and gave vent to a long pent-up giggle. The madness of the post-demonetisation sales had affected her.

'After midnight, 500- and 1000-rupee notes will no longer be legal tender,' a television screen announced, somewhere amidst the din. A clock struck eleven.

'Your bride will be happy when she marries you. Who knows what the future holds?' the old lady speculated.

'I agree, Mother,' he replied, as he extracted sixteen packets of brand-new 1000-rupee notes. It was a sign of the times, and of the fervour of that night of 8 November, that she did not count the money. Instead, she bounced and weighed the wads in her hands before secreting them away in the locker from which she had extracted the gold.

Back at home in the flat, he felt the urge to count his treasure. His once treasure from the heist, the biggest in his life, that he had so painlessly executed over Diwali. On Sunday, 30 October, he had broken into the house of the mistress of a recently retired civil engineer.

Gunvanti Devi was a flirtatious young lady of Ghaziabad, who lived just two floors above him. Her benefactor, Arjun Singh, was a cousin of the infamous Kumar Yadav, who had been arrested when the police discovered a cache of diamond-studded gold in his Audi Q7. Four kilos of diamond-encrusted gold bars.

Arjun Singh had not been so flashy. He invested only in a beautiful and good-natured mistress, having married off his daughters and settled his sons.

The building chowkidar had kept Raju abreast of neighbourly gossip. Gunvanti had suddenly left for Benares as her mother had expired.

The rest was a cakewalk. An empty flat, and a moonless Diwali night illuminated with flashing rockets and bombs and sparklers. The swirling mist of fumes from the fireworks gave Betaab a cloak of invisibility. He went into the flat only at 3.45 in the morning, after consulting the *panchang*, the almanac, for an auspicious time.

It was, after all, the Festival of Lights, the sacred night of Diwali, and he was in a way, in *his* way, worshipping the Goddess of Wealth, paying obeisance to her.

He had not been greedy, he had not taken all her cash away. Just enough to set himself up for a lifetime, or at least a few long years.

Gunvanti had left on 28 October, two days before Diwali. She wouldn't be returning until after all the funeral rites were over. He calculated that she would be back after the final prayers of the thirteenth day.

And what would she do then? What indeed? She couldn't go to the police and complain that Kumar Yadav's loot, siphoned off to his cousin Arjun Singh and devolving on her, had been stolen ...She could be arrested for that. And now Modi-ji, their esteemed prime minister, had dealt them both a double whammy. The money, extorted with savage skill from rapacious builders and corrupt cement dealers, had become just paper.

Well, he had the gold, and he would deal with the rest, with or without Modiji's blessings.

He encountered Gunvanti Devi in the lift the very next day, accompanied by an elderly female relative. The young woman looked heartbroken, but in the way of someone who had lost a much-loved parent; she seemed not to have yet registered the theft, or the impact of demonetisation on her life. He conveyed his condolences with a gravity befitting a concerned neighbour, and kept a lookout for her protector Arjun Singh, who would surely surface soon.

The poet in him had not been left unmoved by the ways of fate and politics, and by the consequences of human greed. He could see himself quite clearly for what he was, a common thief, but he could also recognise the thieves he thieved from. He wrote a long poem on this, titled 'Chornama', extolling the (imaginary) woman who had stolen his heart, addressing the ultimate thief, puzzling about the ownership of love and life.

'He who gives of life/He who steals the gift he has imparted.'

He wrote the poem late at night, with Prime Minister Modi-ji's words still ringing in his ears. But it was money that paid the bills, not philosophy or poetry. He went to the bank to change money while it was still legal to do so, but the queues were too long and too desperate. The grocer changed some money for him, at a percentage. He resisted counting the stolen money hidden in the bathroom; he was stubbornly superstitious about this, convinced that something bad, something even worse, would happen if he began lamenting over the now invalid notes.

There was panic and hysteria on the streets. The rules kept changing, with the finance minister coming up with contradictory statements and absurd restrictions. There were no new notes in the banks, or in the ATMs. People went around carrying change in shopping bags, exchanging IOUs, bargaining and bartering.

Betaab found Gunvanti Devi weeping in the lift. He tried to console her, awkwardly and sincerely. A widow who lived up on the fourth floor jumped off the balcony and died. She had just sold the flat she lived in, and was left with a heap of worthless cash she could not admit to. It was a world that had lost any semblance of normality. Betaab was a worried and confused man, when he decided to consult the wisest man he knew.

Dada Sadarangani had a shop in the Atta Market, where he sold second-hand textbooks, and old magazines and paperbacks. This was just a side business, as he had an affection for words, for books and literature. His real business was that he was one of old Delhi's most entrenched and influential *kabadiwalas*. He bought garbage, sold garbage, recycled garbage. All the leftovers and debris of urban life were skilfully recycled. He took the refuse of the city and transmuted it to gold.

Dada Sadarangani's family had fled from Sind, Pakistan, during the upheavals of the partition years. His brothers and cousins relocated to Bhopal, but he insisted on staying on in Delhi, without them. Delhi was the city of poets, of Mir, and Ghalib, and Dada was in love with the Urdu language, with the feel of its words, with their multiple meanings and their playful way of saying so many things at the same time.

Young Sadarangani adopted the pen name Alfaz, and wrote poetry in the long nights, in the small and airless room he had rented. He also distributed newspapers, in the mornings, and worked as a kabadiwala in the day. His canny Sindhi instincts guided him well, and soon he was a wealthy man, liked and respected by all who knew him.

It was in the second-hand bookshop that he and Betaab had first met. They were drawn together by a mutual love of poetry, and each quickly recognised the other's worth. They became friends. Perhaps Dada Sadarangani was the only true friend Betaab had ever made.

Raju went in a taxi to the shop in the Atta Market. Dada could sense his tension, and led him to the sheltered alcove behind the bookshop that opened into a small walled courtyard where only the whirring pigeons could hear them. Raju told him, tersely, that he had some money, and he didn't know what to do about it.

'How much?' Dada asked cautiously. He didn't care to know about other people's financial affairs, or to disclose anything about his own.

'I don't know,' Betaab replied absently, 'perhaps thirty to forty lakhs. Maybe more. I haven't counted it properly. And it's not clean money.' Dada understood the subtext and didn't probe any further. His business as a kabadiwala involved a complex and sophisticated degree of financial recycling at different levels. His eyes lit up as his nimble mind came up with an impeccable idea.

'Today, I will speak to you not as Raju but as the poet Betaab,' he said. His eyes were gleaming with mischief. Raju had no idea what he meant, nor why he was joking about such a serious matter, a matter of life and death, really.

Dada Sadarangani outlined his scheme. It was a simple idea, with no glitches in it. He, Dada Sadarangani - in this case the poet 'Alfaz' - and his bookshop would make the poetry of Betaab available to the world, at the cost of 90 rupees a copy, to be published by Alfaz Publications. They would, notionally or otherwise, print and distribute this volume, or these volumes, of poetry, and send them out through Dada's network of newspaper vendors and ragpickers that had its spreading tentacles across Uttar Pradesh and the heartland of India.

'Not for nothing am I known as the Master of Jugaad! I began life as a kabadiwala. I have studied in the School of Life, and in the University of the Footpath. We shall transform your poems into banknotes. We shall recycle the black money which you got from god-knows-where and wash it in detergent and convert it into the purest proudest white money. We shall make you into an intellectual, brother Raju, a Buddhi jeev, a Kaviraj.'

He stopped for breath, then began again, the light of entrepreneurial conviction in his eyes as he stroked his grey-stubbled chin. 'It's a dream scheme! Each book will be priced at RRP of 90 rupees but ultimately sold to the customer, the reader, at a discount for only 10 rupees. No remainders, no returns and no receipts. So if we sell 50,000 copies of your book, even to ourselves, we can tell the taxman - and Mr Modi and Finance Minister Mr Jaitley - that we have legally earned 50 lakhs, less publisher's fees, with Alfaz keeping 20 per cent. I have other customers who would be interested in cooperating with you. Life is very simple, really, if you look at it the right way.'

They worked hard on the book, pouring their hopes and emotions into it. They would discuss it late into the night over innumerable cups of strong sweet tea, and agreed to title it *Waqt Chor, The Thief of Time*. They downloaded an Urdu font called Nastalique and hired someone to key it in. Dada procured an ISBN number for the book.

'Raju Srivastava is a useless name for a poet,' he had declared. 'Why, I have seen a comedian with a silly smile, and the same name, on television.'

'I could became Razi Khan Singh,' Betaab replied. 'It's Muslim and Hindu and sounds noble and aristocratic.'

The first print run was of a thousand copies. To their surprise it sold out, quite legitimately, and was reviewed in two Urdu journals of repute.

There was a careless inevitability in the sequence of events, a divinely ordained synchronicity in their unfolding and dovetailing. Raju effectively laundered the cash which he had stolen from Gunvanti Devi, who was holding it for Arjun Singh, who had siphoned it off from his cousin Kumar Yadav, who had blackmailed construction companies, guilty of playing with specifications and diluting cement and propping up soon-to-collapse buildings and flyovers with sand masquerading as cement.

It was almost like the Tree of Life. All the bad karma transformed by the power of the word, the printed word, the virtual word, into legitimate tax-paid income. Raju the thief had sponsored the poet Razi Khan Singh Betaab - and a new narrative had been born.

And now here he was, at the festival, dreaming of the morrow when he would leave his book for Janaab Javed Akhtar Saheb, in his room, or at the hotel reception, signed with all humility and reverential adoration.

Jaipur, January, Saturday

In the authors' lounge, Anirban came across Gayatri Smyth Gandhy. She hadn't been able to keep away from the festival, away from a possible chance encounter with Sumedh. She was introducing herself to a balding man and Anirban caught the name.

'I am Gayatri Smyth Gandhy,' she said in a cool, precise voice. He knew the name. He had encountered her in email loops, in petitions, he had seen her books. They shared an agent. He waited until she had moved away from the balding man and then approached her.

'I think we share an agent,' he said. 'I am Anirban M., and Cathy Cuthbert speaks of you often.'

Gayatri Smyth Gandhy looked pained at the mention of her agent. She needed somebody who believed in her, supported her, someone who could sell her rights. Cathy Cuthbert was not that person. No doubt she was at the bottom of Cathy's list of priorities.

'Cathy Cuthbert is a wonderful agent,' she said stiffly. 'I'm so happy she represents you. As for me, I'm looking forward to becoming a real writer. I've been just an academic so far, writing from my ivory tower, I'm afraid.'

Anirban M.'s artist's eye examined her acutely. She was slim and supple, and seemed to have worn well for a woman in what he guessed was late middle age. Her eyes dominated her face, as did her full lips, which were a bit chapped with vestiges of lipstick in the cracks. He searched for that feature he would accentuate or play with if he drew her, and decided it was her clearly defined eyebrows, and the tiny mole on her chin which accentuated the full lips. She could do with some more consistent make-up, and then she would be very pretty indeed.

He would have been surprised to discover how closely his thoughts echoed Gayatri's own new-found resolution to 'do something' with herself. That inexplicable encounter with Sumedh Kumar, their escape from the hospital, the night they had spent together in her hotel, the kiss he had planted on her lips at dawn, the size and colour of his wife's teeth ...these things had combined in her heart and head and left her determined to get a total makeover, and to steal back the affections of her once-upon-a-time lover.

She had not encountered Sumedh since his silent exit from her room. Yet they were bound to meet; she would see him again, remind him of all that he had lost, and how little he had gained in marrying Anita Husain, and even less in being tied in matrimony to Carmen Kumar. Cupid and Kamadeva would align to help her.

A helpful volunteer was hovering around, clearing away the empty coffee cups. 'Where can I buy some Rajasthani fabric - georgette and chiffon saris, lehariya, bandhej, that sort of thing?' Gayatri asked her, turning away from Anirban.

Anirban overheard her. 'I'm going sari shopping myself,' he said. 'Why don't you come with me?'

So they set off together, Gayatri Smyth Gandhy and Anirban, into the pink city to plunder its treasures. She remembered a childhood trip to Jaipur, arriving with her aunts for a cousin's wedding, and the fervid trousseau-shopping expeditions that had preceded it. She had been enchanted by the burnished *gota*, the gold and silver borders, the fine georgettes, the tie-and-dye *bandhinis*, and the riot of colour that seemed to compensate for the muted arid landscapes and the rich but monotone ochre of the desert dunes.

In a sari shop in a rundown shopping mall, Anirban ordered the assistant to lay out the saris in two neat rows. Then he stepped back, one step, two steps, until he could get a sense of perspective. He settled himself in a dusty white plastic chair and gazed at the display in silence, taking in the colours, feasting on them.

'Searching for a beautiful sari is an immersive experience,' he explained. His face was cupped in his hands, and his eyes had a strange glaze to them. 'Which one do you like best?' he asked Gayatri.

Her gaze settled on a green sari, a bright forest green, with a saffron border and orange tie-and-dye circles around its body.

'This one,' she said, draping it around her shoulders, feeling the sinuous flow of the fabric.

'Nah!' he responded. 'Parrot green is not your thing.'

He was right, of course he was right, the colour was much too sharp. 'Let me look again,' she said, and they continued to stare at the saris, mesmerised by the power of the colours.

A group of women, clearly wealthy and intent on purchase, entered the shop. 'We want wedding saris!' they declared.

The shopkeeper gestured to the assistant to move the display aside and make way for the new customers. The youngest in the group, perhaps the bride-to-be, stopped him and pointed to the palette of colours Anirban had laid out. 'This looks like a good selection,' she said decisively. 'Let us look at these ones first.'

Anirban M. leaped to his feet. He picked up a deep maroon sari in a striking lehariya pattern, with a delicate copper and gold border and a magnificent *pallav*. He draped this around the young woman, then stepped back to examine her. 'This one is meant for you, and you alone,' he declared.

She smiled delightedly. 'You are right, bhai saheb,' she said. 'I will wear it for the Mehendi.'

He then selected a pale pink sari with a sheer silver border. 'This one is for you, Gayatri,' he said decisively. 'It is a pure *pyaazi* colour, a pale onion pink, and not everyone can carry it off.'

She caressed the sari, delighted by his choice. It made her feel beautiful just to hold it.

'And this one is for me,' he continued, sweeping down to gather up a magenta sari with a dramatic pink border.

Gayatri lifted an eyebrow. 'For your girlfriend?' she asked. 'Or are you married?'

'It's for me,' he said, utterly serious. 'I love the purple spectrum. Lavender, lilac, orchid, fuchsia, plum, mauve, magenta - those are my colours. And this exquisite pink border! This is, after all, the pink city. It was Diana Vreeland who said that pink is the navy blue of India. I think purple is really an excess of pink.'

Gayatri didn't know quite how to respond.

'Are you aware,' he went on, 'that colour is a creation of the mind? It's the effect of electrical impulses on the retina. So, there can be two entirely different perceptions of colour. Just like sex.'

She was shocked, though she tried not to show it. Of course, there was nothing wrong with cross-dressing, she told herself. But saris were meant to be worn by women …

'I love saris, and dhotis,' he confided. 'One is not born, but rather becomes, a woman. Femininity is a magnificent construct and a sari is the most innovative and free-flowing garment in the world.'

'Too much explanation, Anirban,' she said. 'Thank you for finding my sari, and the magnificent backstory.'

'We still have to buy blouses and petticoats for our saris,' he said sagely. 'And then the bangle sellers and the jewellers await our visit!'

Gayatri was not the only one going sari shopping. As they left the shop they bumped into Sumedh Kumar's wife, Carmen, dressed in high-waisted trousers and silver sneakers.

She looked Anirban M. up and down, and gave Gayatri a grimace that could have been interpreted as a smile by a charitable recipient. 'Sari shopping?' she asked brightly. 'So am I. I have decided to buy a chiffon sari. It's time I went native.'

Gayatri responded with a grace she did not know she was capable of. 'You should have got Sumedh to come along and choose it for you,' she replied sweetly. 'I'm sure you will look lovely in chiffon. My friend Anirban helped me find the most divine colour.' She smiled again, holding on to Anirban in a proprietorial way, and marched out.

It troubled Betaab that although he wrote romantic poetry, he did not know any women. Had not known any girls, in fact. How could he? Both his older sisters had married early, and died early.

Women used to come to the tailoring shop in Kanpur and be measured there. His father would tread back a few steps and assess them clinically, detachedly, as though they were wooden mannequins, even if they smelled of perfume or of sweat, and had dabs of kohl in their eyes or bright lipstick that smudged their teeth. He would reach for the worn inch-tape kept always in his right pocket, what he called his *inchi-tape*, and proceed to carefully measure the women who came to his shop, wearing a blank expression on his tired face, conscientiously evading any eye contact.

But Betaab himself never got to really know any women. He went occasionally to prostitutes, and masturbated with monotonous regularity, but the exaltation of the spirit, the poetic union that he craved, was denied to him.

He was determined to fall in love, to meet the woman of his dreams, at the festival. Among the thousands of attendees there had to be a Hindu Kayasth girl who was interested in poetry. A girl who had come there not just in the hope of a selfie with a celebrity, but to share in the world of imagination, in the love for words.

Perhaps she was not a Kayastha, or a Hindu. Perhaps the girl he was destined to meet awaited him in a *gharara* or a sequinned salwar kameez. Perhaps she was named Ayesha, or Firdaus Begum. She would speak Urdu with an elegant accent and the correct inflections. He could marry her; he would have no problems marrying a Muslim girl. Kayasthas were a secular, an enlightened community ready to take the best from all streams.

He was infatuated already but it was with a language, the *zubaan*, the tongue of Mir and Dagh and Ghalib. He didn't think much of the revolutionary poets. Although Faiz Saheb's love poetry sent him almost into a state of inebriation, the revolutionary writers and the *inquilabi* progressives left him unmoved.

Betaab examined the printed programme, which he had marked extensively with dots and squiggles. He wanted to take in all the poetry he could, in whatever language. There was a session by a hip-hop poet from London - a stunningly beautiful woman with golden hair - and a Somalian-American rap artist from New York. The presentation of *firangi* poetry was very different from the stylized *andaaz* of the Urdu world. He was curious, he wanted to understand the ways and wiles of the spoken word.

The closing session of the day was the poetry hour. Seven poets from around the world would read from their works. Perhaps he too would be there one day, among them, mouthing each word as though it were a flower or a pearl.

Betaab set off on this winter day in pursuit of poetry and love. He took an auto-rickshaw, but the crowded traffic was frustrating and after a while he asked to get off. Wandering around aimlessly, playing in his mind with a line of poetry that had pushed into his consciousness, he found himself in a beautiful park with green lawns and shady trees.

He sat down on an iron bench, spattered with bird droppings, then got up and settled himself under a spreading peepal tree. A crow hopped around, examining him curiously. A frayed yellow kite fluttered down and fell into his lap. It was just a week or so after Makar Sankranti, and the Festival of Kites had left its annual debris of torn and mouldy paper kites, of all colours, nestling in branches and electric wires across the city.

But the way in which this particular kite, with its faded yellow body and purple heart, had hovered over him before landing on his lap, started a sort of electric storm within him. It was as though this abandoned kite, its wasted skeleton, was speaking to him, and to him alone, about its lonely flight and its return to earth, of the joyous winds and the sorrow and redemption of mud and leaves.

The words that had been stuck somewhere between his heart, and his throat, and his eyes, came hurtling out, like silent lightning. He began tapping out the poem on his smartphone frenziedly. He wrote it in Roman script, a cascade of words and feelings.

The poem was in Hindustani, not in Urdu. It was a set of verses really, all addressed to the tattered kite, and then the kite's replies, proud, philosophical, laconic.

It was as though he were in love with the kite. No person or object had spoken to him like that before, with such tenderness, with such a plea for acceptance.

Betaab did not know how long he took to write *Kati Patang*, 'The Fallen Kite', taking its title from a popular Bollywood movie. It emerged in one long flow, without hesitations or corrections. When it was done he could scarcely remember what he had written, or register its quality, whether it was good or bad. He felt only an incredible sense of lightness in his being. He was whistling what seemed a once-familiar tune. It was of course the song from the evergreen film whose title he had so serendipitously borrowed. There had been an alluring widow dressed all in white - Asha Parekh? - and Rajesh Khanna at the very height of his charismatic glory. That was all he could remember of it, except that it was shot in Nainital, against the backdrop of the lake and the mountains.

He looked at the kite, the inspiration for his incredible poetic flight. He couldn't just leave it there, to be thrown away as garbage. He picked it up tenderly and took an auto-rickshaw back to his hotel, where he placed it over his suitcase, a friend that had fallen from the sky.

'There's more to life than books,' Gayatri Smyth Gandhy said to herself as she laid out the georgette sari and its matching blouse on her bed. There was nothing that made her feel as feminine as the soft drapes of a sari. It was too much of a chore to iron and maintain the six yards of fabric in the States, but on the rare occasion when she did, the effect was always a knockout.

There was a session today, on 'The Historical Imagination'. Gayatri was on the panel with Sumedh Kumar. She was looking forward to seeing him again, with or without his wife. She would make an impression on him, with her beauty, her intellect and her wit. They would pick up the threads of their passion again.

Gayatri and Sumedh. Sumedh and Gayatri. They had felt like one person, all those years ago -like the yolk and white of one egg. Even their breaths would syncopate, when they lay down together. They had loved the same films - *Pakeezah*, *Sholay*, *Lagaan*. They admired the same historians - Eric Hobsbawm, Romila Thapar, Bipin Chandra. They disapproved of the Emergency, were ambivalent about the nuclear tests. She only pretended to agree with him on Kashmir; with her father being in the army, she had a different take.

They were, if anything, too close to one another. Sumedh and Gayatri. They could complete each other's half-finished sentences. They shared the same tastes, the same prejudices, held complementary views and validated each other on every subject.

They had almost begun to blur into each other. It should have come as no surprise that Sumedh had dumped her for her best friend Anita, who was everything that she, Gayatri, was not. 'Somehow, the spark has gone missing between us,' he had told her, quite unapologetically.

Sumedh Kumar had been the love of her life, and after he dumped her she had landed, on the rebound, in the arms of Carlson Smyth, a depressive professor of philosophy with an angelic disposition which gave way to occasional bouts of manic rage. It was only after two years of marriage, when they seemed to have settled into a relatively harmonious relationship, that he confessed he was not yet divorced from his first wife, a Gabonese anthropologist who had borne him two children.

'We had moved away from each other,' he explained. 'We had both moved on. I must stress, my darling, that it was as good as a divorce.'

Carlson's wife, Francine Smyth *née* Brazza, was in touch with Carlson about her work. She had written to him recently, and he had gone to visit her in the university town where she now lived. She was recovering from cancer, and there was a chance she would not make it.

'She looked so different!' he exclaimed. 'So wasted. I almost didn't recognise her.' She wanted to move back in with him, he told Gayatri, and for him to look after their children if she died.

'Perhaps we could all live together here,' Carlson said, hopefully, pleadingly. 'We could move to a house with more bedrooms.'

Gayatri did the honourable thing and walked out of their non-marriage. His wife, Francine, died the next year. Carlson pleaded with Gayatri to return home, to be a mother to his children. But she didn't. She couldn't.

However, she continued with the double-barrelled name as she felt Gayatri Smyth Gandhy carried more gravitas than just 'Gayatri Gandhy'. Besides, she didn't want people to know the whole sad and sordid story and feel sorry for her. She had left them behind, those years with Carlson Smyth and their unravelling.

Sumedh Kumar would be on the panel with her, discussing 'The Historical Imagination'. She would take it from there, forgetting the past, moving into the future. Or at least the present.

She hadn't thought of Carlson in a long time. The brooding flashback had disturbed her, left her feeling anxious and acidic. She brewed herself another cup of tea and slowly, very slowly, began reciting her anti-anxiety mantra.

'This too shall pass,' she told herself, in the soothing voice of the banker-turned-Buddhist nun who had guided her through that particular crisis.

She walked over to the mirror and began talking to herself in a soft, hypnotic voice. 'Dear Gayatri,' she said. 'Dear Gayatri, remember that you have everything going for you. But *everything*. You are a successful woman, a respected academic. You are in good health, looking and feeling good. So what if you can't finish your novel? So what if you don't have a man in your life? So what if you are so lonely you want to weep? SO WHAT!'

She stopped herself. This wasn't working. She gave the face in the mirror a determined smile, and then searched in her medicine pouch for an anti-anxiety pill. A glass of water and a gulp, and she felt better already. This too shall pass. All things must pass.

She returned to the mirror and began working on her face. A base, then a mix of two foundations to get the right shade. Shadow and eyeliner, which she removed. Kohl. Lipstick. And then the draping of the sari, tucking it in and wrapping it around, the five pleats, the pallav thrown over her shoulder, concealing yet revealing her slim curves.

'Trouble, here I come!' Gayatri Smyth Gandhy said to the face in the mirror, and gave herself a naughty wink before she set off for the festival.

But she felt like breakfast. The tea and the biscuit hadn't been enough. The dining room was overflowing with familiar faces. Two women she didn't recognise waved and smiled at her.

Instant coffee, parathas, jam and toast, croissants, poha, guavas, bananas, apples were on offer. She had a pot of masala tea and toast with jam and settled down at a corner table. Avoiding eye contact, she checked the incoming emails on her iPhone. She went through her notes for the session.

There was a shuttle service from the hotel to the festival venue. She was shepherded into a taxi with two men, who seemed to know her. As they navigated the chaotic morning traffic, Gayatri clicked on her inbox again. It contained a new email, from Neil Smyth. Neil Smyth: her husband's son. Carlson's son. Francine's son.

Dear Gayatri (if I may)
This is to convey some rather sad news. My father Carlson Smyth (to whom I understand you were very close) is no more with us. He died last week of self-inflicted gun wounds.

My brother Sam passed away last year, and with my father's tragic demise, I am left alone in this world.

It is my solemn duty to inform you that you are the sole beneficiary of my father's will, apart from a generous and adequate bequest in my name.

My father's lawyers shall be in contact formally about this. I thought it best to be in direct communication and share this information with you.

Due to the nature of his death, a post mortem had to be conducted. I will inform you about the details of the burial soon.

Yours in Grief
Neil Smyth

Gayatri's eyes had blurred over and her head was buzzing. The taxi had halted outside the festival, but she was frozen, unable to move, unable to step out. There was a commotion outside. The stalled car was causing a bottleneck near the heavily cordoned gates. A policeman was making angry faces through the glass window and waving his baton at them.

The two strangers in the car treated her with exquisite courtesy. They nudged and pulled her out and led her through the crowds. She followed, in a trancelike dream, then stepped to the side of the road to vomit into the gutter. There was her breakfast, the tea, the toast, the jam, and then waves of empty retching that brought tears to her eyes.

But she did not weep. What she felt was not grief, or sorrow, but horror, and shock - a scream from her past that had followed her against the wind.

She was led into the authors' lounge and given a strong cup of coffee with an extra dose of sugar. A young girl knelt down before her. 'Please tell us what the problem is,' she said. 'Only if you want to, that is.'

The two men from her hotel, her companions in the taxi, were shadowing her still. They introduced themselves, gently, unobtrusively. One was a Parsi poet, Homi Karanjawala. She had heard of him, of course she had. The other mumbled out a name she could not comprehend and sat silently after that, examining his sandals with a perplexed expression.

She was dry-eyed, she could not weep. She sat and grieved for a while, and then, just as suddenly, snapped out of it. She read through her notes for the session, and awaited the arrival of the other panellists. For Sumedh Kumar. She needed a familiar face, a body she had known.

The session was predictable and unexciting. Everybody maintained their expected positions, and the atmosphere was rife with acrimony and mistrust. The right and the left had variant takes on history and the organisers had scrupulously ensured that all points of view were symmetrically represented.

Sumedh Kumar concluded his observations by quoting Romila Thapar. 'History is not written by committees but by individual historians,' he said, 'and in quoting our foremost Indian historian Ms Romila Thapar, I use this opportunity to publicly condemn those who demonise and vilify her.'

He gave Gayatri a tender look while he said this. She had been taciturn and withdrawn throughout the heated conversation, but the other speakers were far too busy pushing their points of view to notice a rather silent woman.

Later, Sumedh held her hand and helped her down the steps as they left the stage. 'I need to talk to you,' he said, whispering so close into her ear that she could almost feel his tongue there.

Her body felt stiff and wooden and her mind was numb. 'Yes,' she said mechanically, 'we must talk.'

'Not in the main authors' lounge,' he said, still whispering. 'Let's go to the other one, behind the main stage.'

And indeed there was a large room, an empty room, where they could be alone.

'Well, what did you think of the session?' he asked brightly.

'Well, you were very good,' Gayatri replied, with utter sincerity but nevertheless in response to the unspoken cue. Sumedh had always been needy of praise, and susceptible to it.

'You think so? Really?' he said. 'I felt I was a bit off-key. That point I made about history as a rallying point in times of societal and political insecurity - that fellow from Yale didn't give me a chance to expand on it.'

Gayatri was observing him with almost clinical detachment. What a vain little man he is, she thought to herself, and how utterly self-centred. He cannot even observe or notice my pain. How could I ever have loved him?

But he *had* noticed that something was amiss. 'Gayatri, my darling Gayatri, why are you so silent? Why are you so sad?' he enquired lovingly.

'Well, I just got the news that my husband - my ex-husband - has died. He took his own life, shot himself. It was a bigamous relationship so I suppose we weren't even properly married.'

That threw him. He fell silent for a while. She didn't feel the need to say any more.

'My dear girl,' he said, squeezing her hand. She could feel the shock, the love, the sympathy streaming from him.

'When did you get to know?' he asked. 'When did you find out?'

She handed him her iPhone, with the email on it. He squinted at it short-sightedly, then began tapping his fingernails on the wooden armrest of his chair. Then he read the email again, scrolling down carefully, intently.

'Gayatri,' he said, in a voice that was meant to be gentle, 'this man Carlson, your husband ...your partner ...was he rich?'

Gayatri considered the question. They had always shared expenses. Carlson had no extravagances. He never seemed to worry about money.

'Well, he was frugal,' she replied. 'I liked to pay for myself. He didn't seem to have any financial anxieties.'

'Any liabilities?' Sumedh persisted. She found the question odd.

'We need to find out how much money you stand to inherit,' he continued. 'You need to be proactive about this.'

She was struck by the 'we'. Where was he coming from? Where was this leading?

'I loved him,' she said, her voice quavering. 'In my way. A lot. He hurt me, in many ways. A lot. I don't want to think about money. And I don't want to think of him, of his skull shattered, of his heart bleeding.'

She wanted to weep, but there were no tears to be shed. Had he thought of her, before he killed himself? Carlson had left everything to her. He had not stopped thinking of her. He had not forgotten her. He had continued to love her.

'Honey,' Sumedh Kumar said, 'honey, you have to listen to me.'

'No. I need to be alone, Sumedh,' she said, and she walked out, jostled by the crowds, past the front gates. She found an auto-rickshaw and headed for her hotel. She got her key from the reception and made her way to her room. She walked slowly, very slowly, for some reason counting her steps as she walked.

Sumedh Kumar was waiting outside her room. 'My driver knew a shortcut,' he explained, 'so I got here before you. I didn't want you to be alone.'

'I told you – I really need to be alone,' she said shakily.

'I'll wait outside your door,' he replied firmly. 'I don't want you to be alone.'

Quentin Cripps sat in an ornate and uncomfortable chair in the authors' lounge in the Diggi Palace. He was struggling to communicate with Temsula Kharmawphlang, who was to be in conversation with him later in the day. They were going over the points they would talk about.

It was not that Kharmawphlang did not speak English, or anything like that. On the contrary, it was her awesome erudition and impeccable Oxford diction that had him floored. Her poise, and her stunning good looks, left him feeling somewhat inadequate, even as he admired her slanting eyes and straight black hair. Something about her posture, the way she held herself, reminded him of Maria.

'If I may quote from Ariel Dorfman and Arman Mattelart,' she said, in a musical voice that tinkled like a bell, 'in their book *How to Read Donald Duck: Imperialist Ideology in the Disney Comic*, which critiques Disney's world-view from a Marxist perspective. I assume you have encountered it?'

Of course Quentin knew about the book. It had been incinerated in public bonfires and the entire third print run had been dumped into the ocean by the Chilean navy.

She continued: 'On the entirely subversive nature of the Disney enterprise, the authors say that it is wrong to even whisper anything against Walt Disney.'

She was relentless. 'But I haven't whispered anything against Walt Disney!' Quentin protested. 'I have penned a biography which admires his spirit, his prescience and his genius.'

Temsula Kharmawphlang was not deflected. 'Mr Cripps, I grew up Kohima, in Nagaland, amidst the backdrop of insurgency and the struggle for autonomy and identity. Yet the all-pervading influence of Walt Disney and his capitalist adventures permeated every aspect of our lives. My Mickey Mouse watch was my most prized possession.'

She paused. 'My most prized possession *in those days*. No longer so.'

He opened his mouth to respond, but she got in first.

'The "Apology for Duckology" states …' and she carried on quoting.

What had he gotten himself into? This was turning into a nightmare.

Then Quentin Cripps had a moment of wild inspiration. He opened his battered leather bag and rummaged through it to locate the Minnie Mouse watch he had bought on an impulse in Frankfurt airport.

'This is for you,' he said. 'It's not Mickey Mouse. Or Donald Duck. It's a vintage Minnie Mouse watch, a peace offering on behalf of Walt Disney. He was a product of his times, as all of us are. Do wear it, please.'

Her mood changed. She was delighted. 'Aw!' she whispered. 'That's a really sweet gesture. And what a pretty red strap!'

She bent over to give him a sudden, affectionate hug. He was enveloped in a familiar fragrance. It was like being a caterpillar inside a bouquet of flowers.

'I'll let you off the hook,' She smiled. 'A few leading questions, then one serious one, and we will open up to the audience.'

They made their peace over cups of espresso and made their way to the venue. It was in the Mogul Tent. Quentin climbed up onto the stage to thunderous applause. There seemed to be all sorts of people in the audience, from a saffron-clad guru in the front row to rows and rows of young people and students in uniform.

He began the session with the Disney clip. 'If you can dream it, you can do it,' he declared. 'And all our dreams come true if we have the courage to pursue them. That's what the great man said, believed and practised.'

Temsula moved the conversation to the films, and they dwelled at length on *The Little Mermaid* and its retelling of Hans Christian Andersen. He spoke of Disney's American interpretation of the story, and the Freudian images and motifs it contained in its evocation of the mer-life.

Temsula smiled benignly through his presentation, not contradicting him on anything and providing occasional tactful cues on art and popular culture to pace it along. He got a bit carried away and wandered off the subject into a spirited eulogy to Hans Christian Andersen, the original fantasist, and the genre of the fairy tale. Andersen was the true precursor to Disney, he explained, a writer whose empire of stories crossed continents, cultures and nationalities.

Temsula was tapping on the dial of her red-strapped Minnie Mouse watch to indicate his time was up. But he was on a riff.

'Hans Christian Andersen and Walt Disney both knew how to share their dreams, and both were modern and contemporary in the truest sense of the word. Disney could indeed be considered the spiritual and material heir to Andersen and his transformative quest.'

It was time for questions, and almost half the thousand-strong audience seemed to be flailing their hands in the air to ask them.

The first question took him completely off guard. 'Sir, how are you related to Sir Stafford Cripps?' a faceless voice enquired from the back rows.

'What exactly was your question?' he asked. 'Could you repeat it, please.'

'Are you from the family of Sir Stafford Cripps, of the Cripps Mission?'

'Who was Sir Stafford Cripps and what was the Cripps Mission?' Quentin replied perplexedly. 'Perhaps we could discuss this later, as I cannot see the connection with Walt Disney, the subject of my talk.'

Another question was already being relayed from the front rows. A young Indian with shoulder-length hair and a red bandanna tied across his forehead adjusted his spectacles and hurled his words in a thin screechy voice.

'In your view, how does the Americanisation of stories from non-American cultures contribute to the furthering of American hegemonic powers?'

He ducked that one, bluffing his way through with generalisations about borderless cultures and shared stories.

Now it was the turn of the guru in saffron robes in the front row who had beamed at him throughout the session. 'You said, sir, that it all began with a mouse. Our Indian Elephant God Lord Ganesha sits on a mouse. Would you say this could be the cause of Disney World's auspicious good luck?'

'Yes, certainly,' he replied. 'A very good point ...well worth considering.'

The last question threw him off keel. An old woman with her hair held up in a loose bun addressed him in a commanding voice.

'In your opinion, Mr Cripps, to what extent was Mr Donald Trump influenced by Donald Duck?' she asked.

Quentin's brows knitted together and his close-set eyes looked even more intense than before. 'Every American has been influenced by Donald Duck,' he replied, 'including Mr Trump.'

Temsula gave him a hug as they left the stage. 'So you are a master of Duckology, after all,' she said, winking affectionately, laughing at her own joke.

'Quack! Quack!' he replied, as the crowds swallowed them up and they set off in their different directions.

Later that evening, he tried to call Maria. The time difference was just three and a half hours, but she didn't answer the phone. She never had, since that call last year. He tried again, twice, on the half hour. Her familiar-unfamiliar voice finally answered. 'You are a nice man, Quentin,' she said, 'but I need other things to keep me going. Can't you understand?'

'Why do I write?' That was what the programme had said. 'Where does the impetus to write arise? Is it in the heart or in the mind? Is it the power of narrative, the search for our stories? The need to address the inner self? To make sense of chaos? Or simply vanity and narcissism? Anton Haldar, Maya Chatterjee and Jon Smith discuss the impulse to self-expression with editor and publisher Mark Romanov.'

Betaab's skills with English were basic; he could read newspapers and make some sense of television panels. And now he listened intently to the session, trying to follow the nuances, to understand why the speakers would break into laughter or frowns on indecipherable cues or comments. He had thought the conversation would be truer, more direct, that it would explain why he, and all the people gathered there, wrote, or tried to write, attempting in their different ways to make sense of their lives. But the panellists seemed to be speaking around the subject.

Anton Haldar spoke English in an accent Betaab could comprehend. He listened attentively to his passionate comments.

'All writers are, ultimately, cannibals, consuming their own pain, and that of others - as well as their ephemeral joys - in their sheer appetite for experience, in the need to assimilate, digest and regurgitate it.' He coughed modestly. 'And of course there is the matter of money, the need to earn a living, to pay the bills, which must never be underestimated.'

Raju Srivastava aka Razi Khan Singh 'Betaab' disagreed. That was not why he wrote. He wrote because he was in love with words, with their sounds and extended meanings. He wrote because he was intoxicated by metre and verse, by the way in which the next word in a poem added resonance to the previous one.

He wrote because the Urdu language and Hindustani gave him a star-studded sky under which he could sleep and dream. But he was getting carried away. He did not write for money. He addressed that need more directly, outside the moral universe, appropriating what he wanted, wresting it from the world around him.

'That's why I write,' he told himself. 'I don't know how they do it in English.'

And then, a surprise. The next session was to have featured the Instagram poet Rupi Kaur. Her disconsolate fans were informed that her session was postponed until the last day, as she had missed her connecting flight in Frankfurt. 'Tough luck, folks and fans,' the emcee said, not looking in the least upset by the no-show. 'And now. A SURPRISE! Four lucky poets in the audience are invited to come on stage and read their poems. Your session will be broadcast LIVE and your poems will be beamed across the world wherever poetry is appreciated! HANDS UP, PLEASE!'

No hands went up, at first. The audience was taken by surprise and people were looking around to see what the others were doing. Years of stealth had made 'Betaab' always alert to the scent of opportunity. He jumped up and down, waving his hands enthusiastically, until the emcee summoned him up to the stage.

'Betaab' made a dramatic entrance, bending down low and taking the blessing of the stage, as he had seen poets do at Kavi Sammelans. He looked at the sea of faces before him, and steeled himself, as he did before a burglary, to be in the moment, with every sense, every instinct, every cell of his being. The crowd cheered him on.

Other hands had shot up in the audience but he ignored them; he had no interest in anything except his beating heart, his voice, his poetry. 'I am just a poor boy,' he said, 'an outsider to this world. Don't ask me my real name; don't bother with my real life. In my poems, I am Razi Khan Singh "Betaab".'

He cleared his throat, and began reciting 'The Fallen Kite' in the original Urdu.

*

'I soared, I swept the skies,
In your firm hand,
I rode the winds ...'

He remembered every word of the verses that had come to him as he sat under the tree in the park that morning. He had his phone hidden in his pocket but he didn't need to refer to it even once. The poem rose to the sky, like a falcon, surveying the world below, and then it fell. Lodged in the branch of a peepal tree, it told its story to the poet.

'Betaab' had never read in public before, but it all came to him naturally, the silences where he held his breath and waited for the words to sink in, the rising and falling cadences, the ending, when he read the last line and wiped the tears that were streaming down his cheeks.

The audience whistled and cheered and demonstrated their appreciation. The next speaker, a tiny young woman in jeans, was led up to the stage as Razi Khan Singh 'Betaab' left it, after executing a courteous 'adaab' to the faceless crowd before him. He was shaken by the enormity of what had just happened. It was too much at this moment to listen to any more words, any more poetry. He needed to be alone.

He found himself in the same park where, that morning, he had written 'The Fallen Kite'. He tried to locate the tree where he had sat, but they all looked the same, large, green and spreading. He lay down on the ground, looking up at the branches, imagining what it must be like to be a tree, a branch, a leaf, a bird, a stranded kite.

An ant was climbing up his arm, and he observed it labouring with all the concentration at his command. He was consumed by another wave of restlessness. He wanted to be back in the crowds, amongst people. He returned to the festival and found a seat in the front row at Charbagh, the venue that had only recently had him declaiming on stage. Even the memory of it felt incredible, like a dream, a delusion. And yet it had happened.

A session had concluded and the next one had not yet begun. The stage manager saw him and gave him a friendly wave, then called a volunteer over and whispered something in her ear. The volunteer came down to where Raju 'Betaab' was sitting and welcomed him warmly.

'Greetings, Mr Betaab,' she said in English, then continued in Hindi to inform him that he had won the contest. They had announced his name at the end of the session but he was nowhere to be found. A press conference was to be set up in the press terrace at five o'clock, she told him. Would he attend, and be kind enough to say a few words to the press?

And so he found himself on another stage, a smaller one, facing cameras and newspaper reporters and bloggers. An elegant lady introduced him, congratulating him effusively for winning the impromptu open mic award.

'And so, a star is born!' she exclaimed dramatically. 'Tell us about your poetry, please.'

He coughed modestly. 'I am Raju Srivastava, also known as Razi Khan Singh "Betaab",' he said. *'Ek chhote se shahar ka seedha sada ladka hoon. Aap sab ka mahutaj hoon ki aapne mere shayri pasand ki ...'*

There were a few international reporters, so the lady who had introduced him translated his words. 'I am a simple small-town boy,' she said, 'who is grateful for your recognition and appreciation.'

'Have you ever published your poetry?' a voice from the crowed enquired.

'My humble volume of poetry, *Waqt Chor*, published by Alfaz Publications, has sold very well in Urdu and Hindi,' he replied.

'How many copies has it sold?' another reporter asked.

'Perhaps forty thousand copies?' he hazarded. He had not sat down for some time with Dada for the complicated double accounting, but that was where the figure last stood.

There were gasps from the audience. Some of disbelief, others of delight.

'Forty thousand copies?'

The flash of camera lights.

'Just one line from your book? Please?'

'*Waqt Chor.*' He cleared his throat. 'The title poem.'

'The Thief of Time treads softly.
Beware His silent footsteps .
Forget not, as He gives - so He takes.
For life itself in a stolen gift,
stolen from Time.'

★

Then he was led off the stage in a burst of selfies. There were requests for one-on-one interviews, and for copies of his book.

'Please buy on Amazon,' he said. 'And now I must go. Thank you for your love.'

And so, a star *was* born. The next day, the Hindi and Urdu press was full of him. 'The Thief of Time Steals Hearts at Jaipur', 'Urdu Poet Wins Award' and so on.

The English-language press took no notice, as was expected, though one news service put out an item with the heading 'Urdu Is Alive and Kicking'.

He had rushed out after the press conference to seek a quiet spot to ring his friend, philosopher and guide Dada Sadarangani. The munificent kabadiwala-turned-publisher had been following his protégé's success through the festival posts.

'Opportunity strikes but once, my prince among poets,' Dada Sadarangani had told him. 'I shall book a quarter-page advertisement in the *Urdu Mirror* and the *Dainik Samachar*. And I'm speaking to a radio presenter in Lucknow. He happens to be my cousin sister's son who has borrowed money from me. Never returned it, naturally, but he will run a special show tomorrow about your book, with an Urdu poetry contest built in where fifty lucky winners will get a signed copy of your book. Now take care and sleep well. Don't drink too much. Don't talk too much. And don't fall in love. We are going to be much too busy, this coming year, making you into a star. *Khuda Hafiz*. May God be your guardian.'

*

Gayatri Smyth Gandhy shut the door on Sumedh Kumar, who had sworn to wait outside. She sat down on her bed, closed her eyes and at the same time tried to close out all thoughts, all feelings. Her attempts at deep breathing made her choke up, however, and she realised that, far from calming herself, she was in the throes of a full-blown panic attack. She searched for an anti-anxiety pill from her medicine box and swallowed it. Then, for good measure, she took another. But the pills seemed only to have woken her up, made her even more distraught.

She tried to think of Carlson, to pay homage to him, but found that she couldn't clearly remember what he had looked like. It was as though an eraser had rubbed him out, had robbed her of memory. She googled him and found a photo and an article on an academic site. Spectacles, a nose, a not-quite smile - it could be anybody's face. Anybody at all.

She opened the door and peered out. Sumedh Kumar was still waiting for her. He was seated on a white plastic chair, reading a tattered magazine from a pile that sat on a cane table in the verandah.

'Come in,' she said. 'Do come in, Sumedh.'

He entered silently, cautiously, then put his arms around her, as though to console her. Before she knew it she had turned his face to hers and was kissing him, with a fierce passion that surprised, even frightened her.

She felt salty, and sour, and afraid - and he was hesitant, gentle. She held on to him, as though to ensure that he was alive, and that she was alive, and that their bodies established the world of the living.

Later, they fell asleep in each other's arms.

'I want some tea,' she said when they woke up. But it was much later than she had thought; the evening had set in. They went to the restaurant and had a drink, and another, and revelled in the secret intimacy of lovers.

'My marriage to Carmen - it's unravelling,' he said. 'Our relationship came apart quite soon after we married, but now there's nothing to hold us together. Nothing at all.'

Gayatri didn't reply. She didn't know how to reply. She was trying to journey on from the past. She was trying not to think of Carlson.

'And Anita - your friend Anita,' he went on, 'I was never in love with her. But she came on to me really strongly after you dumped me, and before I knew it we were married. But not for long.'

Gayatri was too tired to react to the irony of it. 'I didn't dump you,' she said. 'You dumped me for my best friend. But it doesn't matter, nothing matters very much ever, even though we think it does. Our past is littered with exes, but I love you, Sumedh, and always have.'

'I love you too, Gayatri,' he replied. 'Let's not talk about it any more before we lose each other again.'

Rudrani Rana had given up on her reveries. She did not want to think about the past. She would not think about the past.

She turned instead to her most beloved of pastimes, on a par almost with her love of writing anonymous letters. She made out lists, of important things, random things, pointless things. To Do lists that provided structure and meaning to long and lonely days spent wrestling with words.

She took out a purple pen and began writing. Then she put it away, replacing it with a green-topped gel pen. Purple was for truth telling.

Five Things To Do Before I Die. She scratched that out and began again. *Six Things To Do Before I Die.*

She let her mind wander.

1) Travel. To Rome, Greece, the ancient world. (As Alfred Lord Tennyson had written: 'For all experience is an arc wherethrough gleams that untravelled world whose margin fades for ever and for ever when I move.')
2) To eat an artichoke (Stella Murch used to talk about artichokes, and how much she loved them. Rudrani had never even tasted one.)
3) To have been my twin brother. (She scratched this out, then wrote it again.) To have been able to know my twin brother.
4) To see the Face of God. (Writing this gave her a deep sense of peace. She smiled as she wrote the line, and closed her eyes for a few minutes to connect with the darkness within.)
5) To win the Man Booker prize. (After careful consideration, she changed this.) To see that day, someday, when the world will recognise my talent.
6) I want to learn to see in the dark. To train my dark-accustomed eyes to vision without lights.

And then she wrote out one more, and her list became Seven Things To Do Before I Die.

7) I want to sail in a storm-swept sea. (She pondered this, and cut a line through it.) I want to be a wave in a storm-swept sea.

'Rudrani, you are getting morbid,' she told herself. 'And also maudlin.'

She set about studying the festival programme, the menu of intellectual delights, for the next day. She marked a few, with her green gel pen. Only one session got a double tick. 'Why Do I Write?'

'Why do I write? Where does the impetus to write arise? Is it in the heart or in the mind? Is it the power of narrative, the search for our stories? The need to address the inner self? To make sense of chaos? Or simply vanity and narcissism? Anton Haldar, Maya Chatterjee and Jon Smith discuss the impulse to self-expression with editor and publisher Mark Romanov.'

She reread it critically and snorted to herself. 'Juvenile!' she exclaimed. 'Just simply juvenile.'

She thought of *UNSUBMITTED*, snug in its canvas bag, the manuscript undisturbed by recent revisions, serenely rereading itself, without the intrusion of other prying eyes.

The enlarging mirror. She held it in her hand. It reflected her face but she did not look at it. 'And why do you write, Ms Rudrani Rana?' she said, her voice mimicking that of an eager journalist.

Then her own voice, again. 'Why do I write? Why do I breathe? Why does the caged bird sing?'

Then the journalist's voice again, anxious to know.

'Would you say that writing is a form of soliloquy?'

'No, my dear,' Rudrani Rana replied, her voice gentler because she sensed the young woman's genuine desire to know, to learn. 'Writing is not a form of soliloquy. Writing is a dialogue with oneself.'

She picked up the canvas bag and took out the manuscript. She held it to her breasts. 'Shh,' she said. 'Shh, they are listening. Keep your silence.'

Stella Murch had loved Tennyson. 'Full many a gem of purest ray serene/The dark unfathom'd caves of ocean bear/Full many a flower is born to blush unseen/and waste its sweetness on the desert air.'

And then there was Thomas Gray's 'Elegy in a Country Graveyard'. 'The poet wanders at dusk through a churchyard cemetery ...' She could hear Stella Murch's tinny classroom voice ringing in her ears.

Stella Murch had loved the poem because Lord Alfred Tennyson had loved it. She had a portrait of Tennyson hanging in her drawing room - her parlour, as she called it.

A long sad face, a wavy beard, a balding forehead framed by thinning hair. 'Who is this?' she had asked the teacher, as she examined the portrait that hung in her parlour.

'Who do you think it is, Miss Rana?' Stella Murch had replied, posing a counter question.

'Is it Rabindranath Tagore?' Rudrani had asked. A long beard. An intense expression. It must be him.

Mrs Murch had laughed contemptuously. 'That Bengali,' she had exclaimed, 'who writes songs about bangle-sellers! No, it's not him. It's my grandfather, girl. My blessed grandfather. Don't you know I'm descended from nobility?'

It was only later, much later, that Rudrani had seen the tiny inscription at the bottom of the frame. *Lord Alfred Tennyson*.

There were no seats left by the time she got to the session. She floated at the edges, listening in, before she found a spot in the front, where she squatted contentedly on the grass.

'All writers are, ultimately, cannibals,' Anton Haldar was saying, 'consuming their own pain - and that of others - as well as their ephemeral joys.'

Jon Smith was quoting Oliver Sacks on the process of writing, its illuminations and its darknesses, waving his red-sweatered arms around in the air. He concluded, 'And I'm sure the speakers on stage, and the perceptive people in the audience, will all agree with me that writing is a psychologically messy process, and yet one which is uniquely satisfying for both the creator and the consumer of the literary work. Sacks used the phrase' (and here his red-sweatered arms again resembled two athletic, semi-circular arcs), ' "autobiographical memory".'

Rudrani rummaged in her handbag for a notebook and wrote it down.

And then it was time for questions. Her hand was, as always, among the first to shoot up. 'You in the front,' the moderator said.

Rudrani got up unsteadily and held the mic close to her face. 'My question is this,' she said. 'Would you say that writing is a form of exorcism? Can it rid us of trauma, or conversely, might it, in some cases, actually reinforce it?'

Maya Chatterjee took the mic. 'That's an excellent question,' she said, 'and it deserves careful consideration. If I may respond, please?' Her voice did not carry the implicit condescension of many of the speakers. Rudrani did not feel she was being talked down to.

'Writers are often tormented by secret fears and desires, which are channelled by the act of writing. Indeed, in many cultures and religions, exorcism is the act of driving off, or warding off, demons and evil spirits. It is a form of ritual utterance, of summoning and rejecting, and is in essence an act of healing, and if I may call it that - of reawakening. So if the exorcism succeeds, if the writing is good, the heart and mind can transcend and move on.

'However, there is another aspect to this,' she added. 'Whoever said that "art is a wound that cannot heal" was correct, since for many of us, our art is exactly that: a pain that will not release us. I do not have an answer to your question, but these are my thoughts.'

Rudrani was scribbling in her notebook again. *'Art is a wound that cannot heal ...a pain that will not release us.*

She floated off to another session, feeling strangely light-hearted and unburdened. It featured a middle-aged woman who had self-published on Amazon and sold an impossible number of a romance-gone-wrong tear-jerker. The writer, Rudrani didn't bother to register her name, was very attractive, with a sculpted body and an arresting face. But her vanity, her shrill self-assurance, offended Rudrani. It's never that easy, she thought to herself, disagreeing with the speaker's words. It's never quite as easy as you make it sound.

She made her way to the secret spot near the press terrace that was her retreat and refuge. She extracted a postcard from her bag, with *Visit Rajasthan* embossed on it, and a row of camels silhouetted against the sunset, the sand dunes shining golden in the evening light. She rummaged for her purple gel pen but it had got lost, or hidden itself, somewhere in her capacious bag. She had to make do with an ordinary ball pen.

'Ms Maya Chatterjee, this is in appreciation of your thoughtful and unprejudiced reply to my question about writing as exorcism, art as healing. Sincerity is a great quality, as is humility, and I commend you for both.' She signed her name with a flourish.

Anirban M. spotted her. He had been watching out for the old lady, wondering where in the crowds she might be adrift. He felt a tug of affection in his heart when he saw her.

'Hello, madam,' he said, giving her an exaggerated salute. 'I see you are at your letter-writing again.'

'It's an appreciative one, this time,' she replied. 'A most accomplished member of the tribe of the young actually replied to my question at a session today without treating me like the troglodyte most people think I am.'

'Who or what is a troglodyte?' he asked her cheerily. 'Not a learned and gracious intellectual like you, surely?'

She smiled back at him fondly. 'I am always wary of charming young men,' she said, 'and anyway there are all too few of them around. Bless you for being kind to an old lady.'

Something had happened to her, during that session. 'Why *do* I write?' she had asked herself, She had recognised something about herself, about the book she had written. It was time to unburden herself, time to move on.

'I have a serious question for you,' she said to Anirban. 'If an old woman who had written a novel gave it to you, asked you to read it - how would you respond?'

Her voice, which he had noted as being sometimes coy, even girlish, was at an entirely different register now. It was earnest, cautiously beseeching.

'If the old lady was the enchanting troglodyte seated before me, I would reply in the affirmative. I would say that I would be honoured to read it,' he replied.

She bent down, picked up her canvas bag and handed it to him.

'My novel,' she said. 'This is the only copy I have, the only updated and corrected one. Don't worry, it's on my computer too, somewhere. Read it when you like, as you like, whenever you have time and the inclination. I've been hanging on to it. It's time to let go.'

He held her hand and squeezed it. 'I know what this means to you,' he said. 'I am honoured by your trust.'

'I need your numbers and address,' she said, 'and I must give you mine.' She took a postcard out of her handbag, this time of the Taj Mahal. On it, she printed her name in capital letters, and her phone number. 'I don't use email much, but you can mail me on *rrana@hotmail.com*,' she said, 'and here's my address.'

He gave her his card, then another, in case she were to lose the first one. Then he knelt down, on the brick floor, and kissed her hand. 'You are a magnificent woman,' he said, 'and I'm sure you are a magnificent writer.'

She got up to take her leave of him. Her feet felt heavy, but her heart once again felt light. 'I must depart this circus of words and egos,' she said, in a mock-serious voice, and left. She made her way to the crowded festival bookstore, but was not tempted to buy anything. She needed a respite from words, a return to the primary acts of living.

And yet a fanciful vision came to her mind, of a book in print, of future festivals, of readings and book signings of her very own *UNSUBMITTED*. Or *The Face by the Window*.

The festivities all around her drew her in, the crowds, the intensity of their involvement with the writers and books being discussed, the young people taking selfies and hunting for celebrities, the old who felt young again in the exhilaration of community.

Rudrani ate an entire plate of crispy puris at a stall run by a lady who looked like a royal princess. She dropped one of the pastries and it fell apart in her hands, leaving her wet and sticky. But she took that in her stride.

It felt strange to be carrying only one bag. She could not believe that she had done that, that she had left her life's work in the hands of someone who was, when all was said and done, a stranger.

She thought of all the mothers of myth and history who had abandoned their children in reed baskets, left them to their fates and the currents of the water. And there were many. In the *Mahabharata*, Kunti abandoned her son Karna in the shallows of a fast-flowing river. The baby Moses in the Old Testament was left in a papyrus basket by the banks of the Nile. In Dehradun, a desperate mother had deposited a baby girl in a paper carton near the laundry room. Her mother had told her about it.

The festival too was a sort of river and her book was safe with Anirban M. 'The kindness of strangers.' She loved that line. Tennessee Williams, *A Streetcar Named Desire*.

What if he pretended it was his book, sold it to an international publisher and it became a bestseller the world over?

'I would still be happy if that happened,' she told herself. 'I am ready to send the book out into the world.'

On that philosophical note she wandered off towards the colourful stalls. A striking purple shawl was on display, a purple shawl with blue and mauve poppies. She couldn't afford it but bought it anyway, on her credit card. Then she left for her guestroom, walking there to save money. She was so used to being burdened with the two bags that it felt unnatural to be holding just one. She could feel the phantom weight of the canvas bag and her book within it.

That night she put off the lights and pretended that she was dead. She shut down her senses one by one. First the eyes, evading the images that rose in the dark. The woman at the stall selling puris, with her regal posture. Her picture rose in Rudrani's eyes although they would never in all probability encounter each other ever again. In this life. She willed the image away and thought of nothing. The ears. Shut down the ears. They could hear the chatter of the two sisters downstairs, and the sounds of television. The nose. It was blocked, the dust in the festival grounds had given rise to an allergy. She could smell nothing, but her nose itched, and her nostrils felt strangely heavy, and wary, as if they knew that she was observing them. The breath. The breath goes first.

Touch. The sense of touch. Her mind was playing games again, and she could feel Rupert Murch's fingers, gentle and hard, on her skin.

Then sleep, which is as death. Death, which is the sister of sleep. Would the words never leave her, in sleep, in death?

Anirban M. was seething. His cousin, Chintan Banerjea (with an 'a' not an 'e'), was about to speak in a panel on 'The Truth of Statistics and Economic Growth'. It was a free world, almost and just about, but Chintan's recent free-fall from left-wing idealist to right-wing pragmatist (if not apologist) had startled and shocked Anirban.

As a child, Anirban had hero-worshipped Chintan; they had played together in cantonment towns across India, in Kanpur and Ambala and Ranikhet, as their parents followed transfers and constant reposting. Chintan had gone on to Harvard and to great things. Anirban followed the path less travelled. He studied dance and choreography, then did a course in digital communication in London. This was followed by a year in Santiniketan, and much angst about his chosen stream as an artist, about his sexual orientations, about his political affiliations.

Anirban's success as a graphic novelist, and of the anonymous *Eye Spye* column, had surprised even himself. He had an agent who believed passionately in his talent, a fair income from books and projects, and a place in the world. Albeit utterly lacking in ambition, he realised that he could be ranked as a success, even if only a modest one.

He came to the Jaipur Festival almost every year to simply drift among the crowds and lose himself in books.

He wasn't looking forward to meeting Chintan again. He still carried a reserve of love from those early years of intense hero-worship. Chintan's feet of clay that had recently emerged hurt him as much as they angered him. He resigned himself to sitting through the session. He didn't know if he had it in him to observe a fallen hero.

Anirban was still carrying the canvas bag with Rudrani Rana's manuscript. He had almost forgotten it at the press terrace, and planned to deposit it safely in his room after the eco-con session was over.

As expected, a phalanx of right-wing economists were confronting a flock of liberal and left-wing practitioners. The lines were drawn, and positions hardened. He walked in late and found a seat in a corner. The session had attracted a reasonable audience, but it was not overflowing.

Chintan Banerjea was centre stage. He had a wisp of grey in his longish hair, and retained that particular air of self-possessed panache that had so drawn the young Anirban.

'...if the QES data are extrapolated to the entire non-farm population,' he said gravely, then unleashed a series of unintelligible statistics that Anirban did not even try to understand. 'It seems that the so-called opposition parties and the craven Lutyens media that supports them will go to any lengths to malign Mr Modi. So-called "statistics" are being improvised in an orchestrated campaign to ...'

Anirban switched off. He noted that Chintan had developed a tiny paunch. No double chin yet. As a cartoonist he was alert to the idiosyncrasies of facial and body language and the giveaways they contained.

He began sketching his cousin. The dramatic streak of grey hair was the obvious place to begin, but it was not the obvious that he was searching for. Besides, when he looked closely, he noted that the wing of grey, like a streak of minor lightning, was simply too perfect to be plausible. It was a trick, a prop to add gravitas to Chintan's already ponderous persona.

The eyes? Chintan's eyes searched the audience, beaming out a well-rehearsed warmth, a practised hypnotism. But that was not new. Even as a young man, Chintan had the capacity to make one feel that he was listening, and responding, to you alone.

Anirban's sketch focused on the hands. They were volatile and full of motion, like windmills or the paper wind-spinners they used to play with as children. He inserted a trail of animated motion into the hands, then constructed the rest of the portrait around them.

They met up for a coffee after the session, avoiding the crowded authors' lounge. They spoke of this and that, skirting the distance, the divide between them by talking of trivial things, family gossip, memories of childhood. Anirban had decided he would not talk of ideology, or morality, or ethics; he would not waste his words in reaching out to someone who was so irrevocably set on the path of pragmatic self-betterment.

But he could not help himself. When it was time to get up and move on, after they had promised to meet more often, after a perfunctory hug, he looked Chintan in the eye and asked him, 'Dada, how do you sleep at night?'

There was no reply. Chintan's eyes went glassy, they glazed over in a way that Anirban remembered well from their childhood. He stared intently at Anirban without really looking at him at all, if that were possible.

Then suddenly he smiled and squeezed his hand. 'Stop being so childish, bro,' he said. 'Will you never grow up?' He gave Anirban another hug, a real one this time. And he was gone.

Anirban made his way to the authors' lounge, remembering to take the canvas bag with him. He was fatigued by the festival, tired of words, of everything around him. At the lounge, he settled in a chair in a corner, glowering at a distant video screen.

A rather beautiful young man settled down on the chair beside him. He had a disarming smile, and seemed in the mood to strike up a conversation. On any other day Anirban would have been keen to respond, to listen in, to take notes. But meeting with Chintan Banerjea had left him deflated, and yes, disappointed, that the hero of his childhood memories had succumbed to the lure of worldly success and become the despicable fraud he undoubtedly was.

He got up and made his way to the toilets and waited patiently in line. A woman who had lost her laptop was having a panic attack that bordered on hysteria. 'Oh my God!' she wailed. 'Oh my good lord! Oh my fucking luck! So help me God!' There was a lyrical cadence to her laments. Was she a poet?

He was about to step outside when the beautiful young man called out to him. '*Hellooo,* my friend,' he yodelled from across the room. 'You have forgotten your bag!' He was holding on to Rudrani Rana's canvas bag, containing the manuscript she had so trustingly given Anirban. He felt like a heel. How could he be so careless, so thoughtless.

Anirban immediately went back and introduced himself. Thanked the young man. Explained the circumstances of the bag, and how a reticent author had entrusted him with her life's work. How it was his duty to read it, to assess it, to help it find its way into the world.

The young man introduced himself in turn. It transpired that he was an editor, a translator and a poet. He was also a scout for a famous literary agency. His name was Juan. Juan Torres.

Anirban scratched at his curly hair. 'Everybody around here seems to be a poet,' he said, beaming his seductive dimpled smile at the angelic vision before him. 'I would love to read your poetry - perhaps I could even help you illustrate some verses. And if you are a literary scout, cub, elf, maybe you could even read the magnificent Rudrani's magnum opus?'

Juan Torres had no sessions that day. He curled into a sofa and began reading Rudrani Rana's long and rambling novel. An observer would have noted a range of expressions playing over his face as he leafed through pages in the spiral binding. Amazement, amusement, a whoosh of delight, an occasional giggle - he was reading the book as a child might. He remained glued to the pages for almost an hour before he got up for a coffee and to stretch his legs.

Anirban was waddling towards him, flicking back his long hair. 'Hello yaar,' he said. 'I need to have that baby back, Juan. Can't lose it. It's her life's work.'

'She, whoever she is, is a true original,' Juan Torres responded. 'I can't judge how good or bad it is, but I can confirm that I've never read anything like it in my entire life. How can I meet her, this lady of the poisoned quills?'

'How did you know? How did you guess?' Anirban asked. His mouth had fallen agape in astonishment.

'Know what?' Juan replied, equally baffled.

'That she - my friend - writes poison-pen letters ...for amusement, for truth-telling,' Anirban stuttered.

Juan looked uncomprehending. Anirban registered that the words had been a figure of speech, that he had understood wrongly, inadvertently betrayed a secret, broken a covenant of trust.

'In a manner of speaking,' he corrected himself 'As a metaphor, I meant.'

Juan looked at him with curiosity, then let the matter go. 'I would like to meet her,' he said again. 'I can't put my finger on it, but there is something there.'

Anirban picked up the canvas bag and coddled it. 'I had better be careful with this cute little baby,' he cooed. 'I'm booked for two publishers' parties and an after-party today. Would you care to join me, perhaps?'

A long night, with alcohol and stimulants and laughter, found them in bed together, tenderly spooned into each other's arms. The canvas bag, with *UNSUBMITTED* inside, lay under the bed, like a curled-up kitten or a drowsy puppy.

He woke to the sounds of dawn before falling asleep again. The hoot of a distant train, the cry of a peacock. They had not drawn the curtains, and a faint light filtered into the room. Juan was asleep beside him. His skin felt like, looked like, a pale rose petal.

Anirban felt languorously content, enveloped in a sense of well-being. He knew the feeling. He was falling in love again.

Carmen lay on a flat wooden board, naked. The Ayurvedic massage was her special treat to herself. It was a Jaipur sampler for the fortnight of rejuvenations in Kerala she had booked, after the festival, without Sumedh. The Shirodhara treatment involved having an unfamiliar-smelling oil poured in a thin stream onto her forehead, for what seemed like hours, an eternity almost. It was relaxing, but also in some sense disorienting. And now her body, bathed in oils and unguents, was being pushed and pummelled by two strong women.

She had forgotten what it felt like to be touched. All bodily contact with Sumedh had ceased some years ago. He avoided her, and she had begun to feel a sort of physical repulsion towards him. He was just so …so creepy.

The vigorous massage was making her recognise bits of her body, of her musculature, that she had completely forgotten. Her back, her calves, the insides of her thighs. After a while she drifted off to sleep. In the dark of her mind, lulled by the oil and the incense, she thought - or dreamed - that it was Sumedh who was beating at her body.

'Stop it, Sumedh!' she cried out to him. 'Stop it! I can't bear it!' Then woke up in embarrassment to her own voice. The women therapists were unperturbed, although they had stopped their movements mid-air.

'Sorry, I fell asleep,' she said apologetically, and they began kneading at her body again.

Sumedh had been nicer, more amiable with her during the last few days. She wondered what was going on inside him. He was a complicated person, with almost invisible mood shifts contained in an externally composed exterior. She had never understood why he had proposed marriage to her, and even less why she had said yes.

She concentrated on her body, and how it was reacting to the onslaught of oil and the rhythmic rubdowns. When it was over she felt too lazy to bathe and wash it off in the spartan facilities of the Ayurvedic spa. She returned to the hotel room and zoned off to sleep after eating two bananas from the fruit platter.

The therapist had advised her to detoxify, and she had done so. Yet she awoke past midnight to pangs of devouring hunger. Sumedh had not returned to the room. There was no message from him on her phone. No missed call either. Oh well ...

It took some time for her to fall asleep again. She could smell the pungent odour of coconut oil on her skin. She felt grimy, and yucky, and her sweat glands were blocked.

A miasma of anxiety hung over her. She found herself worrying about their dog - her dog really. Her beagle, Darwin, was with their neighbour and her best friend Louise. Darwin would be wondering where she was, he would be missing her.

She tried to call Louise but couldn't get through. She fell into an exhausted, defeated sleep, until she was awoken by a crash and a loud bang.

It was morning. Her husband, Sumedh Kumar, still in his day clothes of yesterday, was sprawled on the floor. The fruit platter lay shattered, and there was broken china and fruit scattered all around him. A few apples, a pineapple, some chikus, a guava.

She thought he looked like something out of a surrealist painting, and smiled drowsily to herself. Until she realised that he had slipped on a banana skin. One of the banana skins meant for the waste basket but which had landed on the floor. Thanks to her bad aim.

He was furious. 'What are you smiling like that for, you bitch?' he shouted. 'Why is this room stinking of coconut oil? Why have I returned to this conjoined hell?'

She could not help herself. She couldn't stop laughing at the sight of him. She had never actually seen anyone slip on a banana skin. It seemed like something out of a late-night movie.

He lurched towards the bed and began hitting her. He tried to grip her by the wrists, but the coconut oil, still slathered over her, made it difficult for him to hold on to her.

He was not drunk, just very angry. 'You gorilla,' he screamed, 'you ugly gorilla! You left that banana skin on the floor deliberately, so that you could laugh at me! I'll teach you a lesson, you stinking creature.'

By now, her smiles had gone. She was angry, and afraid. She kicked out at him. He picked up the bedside lamp so he could hit her with it. The wire snapped; there were sparks and a flash, a minor explosion.

He sat down defeated on the sofa and started to weep. She tried to soothe him, but it was too late to sound caring. He lay down on the sofa with his shoes on.

'I need to sleep,' he said. 'Don't come near me, you ape.'

'Where have you been all night?' she asked him, suddenly furious.

He didn't reply, pretended to be asleep. She looked around for something to throw at him. The digital watch on the bedside table. She hurled it at him. It missed him and fell on the floor. It did not break.

He opened one eye and looked at her. 'That's it,' he said. 'That's it. I'm moving into another room. You can explain this mess yourself to the staff.'

And he was gone.

Later, she spent hours trying to scrub off the oil with the organic soap, 'handcrafted by village artisans', that the hotel provided. She tried to tidy up the room, which wasn't difficult. A broken lamp, a shattered fruit platter. She could explain those. And a missing husband.

She spent the morning reading a novel, waiting for him to come back. He materialised for a while, packed his clothes tidily into his suitcase, gave her a venomous look, and left again. She said nothing to him. They were through. THROUGH.

Jaipur, January, Sunday

Zoya Mankotia was still agonising about the postcard. 'I feel defiled,' she said, to anyone who would listen to her. 'What sort of person would send me an anonymous letter with a picture of a pussycat on it? Was it meant to suggest anything? Was it a metaphor for my sexuality?'

Maya Chatterjee sat next to her, lending a sympathetic ear. They had spoken, and sparred, in festivals together, and considered themselves allies. Zoya held out the card to her and Maya examined it with interest.

'Hey!' she exclaimed. 'I've received one of those as well. But a nice one.' And she rummaged in her festival bag for the postcard with the camels which had been delivered to her room.

Zoya's face fell when she read it. 'It doesn't help at all,' she said, wiping a tear from her eye, 'to know that you have drawn such a positive response from this person, Maya, while I remain, as ever, the essential bitch. We are what we are, but if we go against the grain, if we are different and ready to defend that difference, we are hated all the more.' She managed a smile, but Maya could see that she was still hurting.

'I wonder who it is,' she said thoughtfully. 'Mine is signed, but quite indecipherable, while yours is anonymous. And they are both in purple ink, in this depressive italic handwriting. She writes, "in appreciation of your thoughtful and unprejudiced reply about writing as exorcism, art as healing". Somebody asked me that question at my session yesterday, and I replied as best I could, but I couldn't really see who it was in the crowd since there was a real crush out there. I think it was a woman, an old woman.'

'Huh! I hope the old hag dies and rots in hell,' Zoya said angrily. 'She deserves to be run over by a car, or trampled by an elephant.' Then she bit her tongue in self-reproach. 'Sorry, I don't know what came over me,' she said in a quieter voice. 'That wasn't nice. I guess I'm the bitch, as usual. What's wrong with me?'

She took the card with the pussycat with the purple ribbon and the purple envelope and put it back in her bag. 'Miaow miaow!' she said. 'I'm moving on. Let's talk of something else, Maya.'

'I'm glad you did that,' Maya responded. 'I do think hurt draws hurt, and pain attracts more pain.' She gave Zoya a hug, and they got down to talking of other important things.

Anirban M. was slouching on the next table, preparing for a session on 'A Sense of the Graphic'. He was half listening in to the conversation. He had watched Zoya as she took out the purple envelope.

'Let it be,' he had advised her silently. 'Perhaps she addressed the letter to herself, not to you. It's her own rage and passion she's projecting.' Yes, best now to let it be.

After his session, which was suitably stimulating and wowed the young audience, he spent the rest of the day with Juan, exploring the familiar city, seeing it through the eyes of another outsider. They went to the Hawa Mahal, and to the Jantar Mantar, and ate jalebis from a roadside stall. Juan confessed that he had always wanted to ride on an elephant, so they went in an auto-rickshaw to Amer Fort where a patient pachyderm lumbered up the incline of the fort, prodded by a bored mahout.

'But this is so humiliating!' Juan exclaimed. 'The most magnificent beast in the world trudging up a hill as a tourist curiosity.'

They disembarked from the elephant, and Juan patted it affectionately. 'You lovely boy, you,' he said. 'Don't let the world get you down. Give it back to them!'

'She, not he, sir,' the mahout said. 'My elephant is a lady.'

'He, she, we - it's all the same,' Juan replied cheerfully. They walked the rest of the way, holding hands, sidestepping pyramids of elephant poo.

In the fortifications behind the ramparts, surveying the city and the hills beyond, Anirban suddenly thought of Rudrani. He had to find her again, to tell her that the first reader of her book had applauded it, that it was stirring to life.

He tried to call her, but there was no network, no signal. He tried again on the way back, from the taxi, but there was no reply.

Anirban got a text message from his cousin that evening. *Let's meet up for a bit before we part again, dear cuz*, it said. Chintan's uneasy use of slang had always irritated him, and he stared at the word 'cuz' for a while.

Yo bro! he replied. *Whenever, whatever you say.* A plan was formulating in his head, whereby he would be able to hold his own in the encounter.

So it was decided that they would meet in the bar of the Hotel Rambagh Palace that evening. Anirban persuaded Juan to accompany him, not a difficult thing to do as the famous Taj hotel was on his bucket list anyway.

Anirban took trouble to dress up stylishly in a black T-shirt and a designer cravat, with a long black shawl to protect him from the distinct bite of the winter evening.

The Polo Bar smelt of wealth, and class, and privilege. It was a compound smell, partly musty, with a whiff of ancient cigar smoke. The walls were cluttered with trophies and memorabilia, crossed swords and faded photographs, the cabinets stuffed with whiskies, single malts, cognacs, wines and liqueurs of every description.

Chintan Banerjea was studying the menu with deep interest. His eyes moved from right to left, frowning at the prices. A thin woman in a chiffon sari and coiffed hair came over to chat with him at his table. Chintan flicked his hair and looked her in the eyes, giving her the full benefit of his dimpled smile.

He leapt forward when he saw Anirban, and gave him a fond hug. He was charming and courteous to Juan, who had introduced himself.

'I'm sticking to a single malt,' Chintan Banerjea declared. 'And perhaps some Asian-style grilled prawns.'

He handed them the menu. A turbaned waiter was hovering around solicitously.

Anirban studied the menu, a mischievous smile lighting up his eyes. Juan observed that Chintan and Anirban had almost identical dimples.

'A bottle of champagne, please,' he instructed the waiter. 'The Dom Perignon, I think, and three glasses. We have something to celebrate.'

Chintan looked disconcerted, and his smile began to look a bit fixed.

'In 1930, the Jaipur Polo team made a clean sweep of all major international tournaments, and this bar was set up to commemorate that unique achievement,' he commented, almost proprietarily.

Juan was still studying the menu. 'That's fantastic,' he responded. Then, to the waiter, 'Perhaps I will have an 1857 Bloodiest Bloody Mary, with Absolut, pepper and wasabi.'

The champagne arrived, and the steward popped the cork.

'This is a special occasion, dearest cuz,' Anirban said, putting his arm gently around Juan. 'I wanted to introduce you to my fiancé - to Juan.'

Chintan looked amazed, then alarmed. His eyebrows shot up, like two inverted arcs, Anirban observed. He was, for perhaps the first time in his life, rendered speechless.

Juan, too, looked amazed, but only for a moment. Then he recalibrated himself, and his face settled in a quiet, rather shy smile, though his eyes held a naughty twinkle.

'Oh!' Chintan said. 'Oh!'

Just then, a famous film star, also a prominent Member of Parliament, walked in. Recognising Chintan, he headed for their table. His body language, despite its natural swagger, was deferential in the extreme.

'I suppose you are here for the literature festival?' he enquired. 'My autobiography is being launched at lunch time tomorrow. I would be honoured if you could join us, perhaps grace the stage?'

Chintan Banerjea had regained his composure, 'Unfortunately, my dear friend, I head back to Delhi soon, where work and duty beckon,' he replied. 'May I introduce you to my cousin, Anirban ...and his partner, Juan?'

The politician left and the grilled prawns arrived. They were delicious. Chintan ate three, then began fiddling with his phone.

'Get him another single malt,' Anirban told the waiter. Then he turned to his cousin, saying, 'Chintan, I'm so delighted to be here with you today. Do you know, Juan, that I hero-worshipped this man throughout my childhood and my youth? I truly believed that the sun shone out of his arse.'

Chintan put another cube of ice in his whisky. He wasn't sure where the conversation was going.

'But he let me down. He let *us* down. He sold out to his ambition, his need to climb the greasy pole. He was my idol, and he turned out to have feet of clay.'

He gulped at his champagne, then held the fluted glass upside down for dramatic emphasis.

'So here he is - mega-successful, ultra-pleased with himself, a right-wing homophobe who endorses genocide and drinks single malt, when really he should be sipping cow urine.'

Chintan's face had turned black with anger. 'I do not really have to engage with you, Anirban,' he said, 'but since we are comparing notes, let me tell you of my assessment of you. An overgrown child, an unfunny clown, a pathetic failure trying to raise laughs at the expense of serious people. You make me want to weep, little cuz, with your leftist affectations and your convenient convictions.'

He stopped for breath. 'Moreover, I am not a homophobe. I believe in life and liberty for all. But I do NOT, in capital letters, NOT believe in irresponsible and unnatural sexualities. What went wrong with you, Anirban? Where did we fail you?'

He turned to Juan. 'I'm glad to have met you, young man, but I must leave now. I cannot sit here to be reviled and ridiculed. I hope Anirban has the wherewithal to settle the bill.'

He swept out of the bar. Juan turned to Anirban to gauge his reaction. His friend was chuckling uncontrollably, holding his belly so as not to roll over from the convulsions of laughter.

'What was that about?' Juan asked wonderingly.

'He was trying to get to me, but I got to him instead,' Anirban replied. 'Victory is mine! Sorry for the misrepresentation of our relationship, but I had to draw him out on all fronts. Why is it that all the ultra-right is homophobic, even if ...' and he broke into another round of giggles.

'May I have another 1857 Bloodiest Bloody Mary, please?' Juan asked. 'And I shall settle the bill. Let this be my treat tonight.'

'I've brought all my credit cards,' Anirban said, still choking with laughter. 'It was worth it, whatever it costs. I wouldn't want to break into your backpacker budget, amigo!'

Now it was Juan's turn to giggle. The absurdity of the evening was getting too much for him.

'It is my pleasure to announce, my dear Anirban, that I am, as you might say in the English, substantially well-off! I happen to be born to a rather distinguished line of plunderers and conquistadors, of different politics and ideologies. So it is my honour, absolutely, to pick up the bill for this highly entertaining evening.'

Anirban looked at him amusedly. 'Beautiful, and rich, and virtuous as well? Maybe we should get married, after all.'

They walked out into the cool night. Anirban pulled his shawl around him and began fiddling with his phone.

'She's gone quiet,' he said worriedly. 'Eleanor Rigby has switched off. I hope she is all right, that nothing has happened to her.'

Nothing had gone wrong with Rudrani Rana, so far, except that she had lost her phone. She discovered the loss when she was walking out of the festival, after the very last session. A turbaned man, wizened with age, was juggling a row of Rajasthani puppets on a bent bamboo pole.

The puppets were turbaned too, and had puppet wives or partners in pretty tie-and-dye robes. Rudrani bought a pair, impulsively, without haggling, without wondering what she would do with them. She tried to stuff them into her big leather handbag, but of course they wouldn't fit, and the puppeteer didn't have a carrier bag to give her.

Her phone rang while she was trying to fit the puppets in - or she thought it rang. She emptied the contents of her bag out in a futile effort to locate it, but it was lost. Of course it wasn't her phone that had rung. They all had similar rings anyway. She must have dropped it, it must have jumped out of her bag, as nobody would care to steal such an antiquated model, such a battered specimen.

She decided to go back and search for it. Rudrani carried a small torch in her bag, always, and she beamed it on the ground as she retraced her steps to the Diggi Palace, slowly, very slowly, retreading her movements of the afternoon.

She kept bumping into people, but she was dogged and determined to find her phone.

But the phone was equally determined to elude her and was not to be found.

Re-entering the festival off-time was a revelation. The crowds had gone, left like a receding tide, and the lawns of the Diggi Palace were relatively empty, with some residents sitting on the lawns, listening to Rajasthani folk music.

There was still an excitement in the air, the accumulated energy of the day slowly dissipating into the chill night. Rudrani pulled her new shawl more tightly around herself, then settled in a corner of the grounds, entranced.

The strains of music from the film *Padharo Mhare Desh* filled the air. *'Kesaria Balam, Padharo Mhare Desh ...'* The rich voice of the singers resonated with lilting joy in the thin desert air. It was a song of the Thar Desert, a song of warriors and lovers, first sung by Allah Jilai Bai in the court of Bikaner.

Rudrani was an assiduous reader of travel guides, and knew this, as she knew about the legend of Dhola and Maru, and so many other important but non-essential facts about things, and people, and words.

She stroked the puppets in her hand and spoke to them in a soft voice, though nobody would have heard her, anyway.

'You are my Dholu, young prince,' she said to the turbaned, moustached puppet, 'and you, my dear, are the Princess Maru.' This to the lady puppet.

She settled them on the seat beside her so they could watch the show, listen to the music. She bought herself some kebabs from a kiosk in the far corner. Then she began searching for her phone again, inch by inch, across the lawn, the driveway, the front gates.

She thought she had found it, when a dog brushed against her, and a motorcycle screeched to a stop. She dropped Dhola and Maru, and had the phone in her hands, when she lost her balance and hit her head against a rock that sat by the side of the narrow road.

Nobody noticed at first that she had fallen over. The dog sniffed at her and walked away. The motorcyclist retreated hastily, without leaving a trace.

A child, a little boy selling *chana jor garam* in newspaper cones, came to her rescue.

'Aunty-ji, aunty-ji, are you all right?' he asked, his small gentle hands stroking her arms as he spoke.

A policeman arrived, and then a wheelchair, and a volunteer. She was taken to a first-aid post near the gate. There was blood over her face, she could taste it on her tongue, rusty, with the texture of mud on it.

'Dhola! Maru!' she screamed, as they wheeled her away. Her phone was in her hand, and her handbag was safe in her lap. At first they could make no sense of her wailing, and continued to wheel her away, but the dusty boy who had rescued her understood her cries, and retrieved the puppets for her.

There were no major injuries, though she needed two stitches on her forehead, and a tetanus shot. She was fussed over, given a cup of hot sweet tea, coaxed to eat a spicy *kachauri*. A taxi was sent for, and she made her way back to her room. The sisters were watching television and did not notice, or chose not to comment on, her dishevelled appearance and bandaged stitches.

She got into bed and laid the puppets down on the pillow next to hers. She felt comforted by their company. Dhola and Maru had watched out for her today. They made up for the aching loss of her manuscript, the absence of *UNSUBMITTED* and the canvas bag.

She checked her phone. There were three missed calls and a message from Anirban M.

'Good night, D and M,' she said sleepily. 'I will call that Anirban tomorrow, A.M.'

*

A dreamless sleep. Her head felt heavy when she woke up, and the crowded sequence of events, of memories and chance encounters that she usually puzzled over when she opened her eyes, were missing today.

And then she drifted off to sleep again. Her mother appeared, surrounded by a halo of light. Her mother, the Matron, Mrs Rana, in her starched white sari, and the small sharp bun at the nape of her neck. She wore her black cardigan over her sari, and Bata school shoes with a strap across them, the same style as Rudrani was wearing. Rudrani too was dressed for school, in a blue pleated skirt, a white cotton blouse and a blue blazer.

'Come on now,' her mother was saying. 'Hurry up, please. It's time to go.' She held Rudrani's hand and led her out into the street, where a high wind was blowing. It was only then that Rudrani realised she had left her school bag behind. She awoke with an intense sense of loss and bewilderment.

She splashed some water on her face, brushed her teeth. Several of her molars were missing, and one felt unusually wobbly today. She took out the bottle of herbal eyedrops and carefully aimed it over her tear-ducts. It was advertised as having a 'natural tear formula'. She liked the thought of that, it amused her. Her vision blurred for a few seconds, and then her eyes could see again.

Her calves hurt, and her knees too, from all the activity of the last few days. A cup of tea and some toast and she would be herself again. Ready to face the day.

She could feel the absence of *UNSUBMITTED*. How could she have given her life's work away to a stranger she hardly knew? What if he got run over by a car? Or abandoned her manuscript in the lawns of the Diggi Palace? And then what if some needy writer found it, claimed it as his own?

She was working herself into a panic. 'How could you be so rash, Rudrani?' she said aloud to herself. She resisted the anti-anxiety pills, they never helped, and instead took ten long deep breaths.

Another, even more terrifying thought struck her. What if the book succeeded? What if it were to get published, what if she were to become a real writer? The idea frightened her. It was surely better never to have tried at all than to be a miserable failure. But to be tested every day by the demands and expectations of prying readers - that was possibly the worst scenario of all.

She searched in her suitcase for The Book. *The Color Purple*. Her guide, her succour through all puzzles and predicaments. She opened it at random and read some lines to herself. Alice Walker to the rescue again. She decided to set off on an adventure. To forget about words and sentences and stories.

What should she do? How would she spend the day? And then it struck her: she would get a haircut! Get rid of the mess of white and grey loose strands that framed her face. Reinvent herself. Be born anew, with a chic hair-do that framed her face like a beret, or a windblown cap.

Rudrani set off with only a hazy idea of where she was going. She wouldn't wander into just any dirty downmarket beauty parlour, she decided. No, she would step into an upmarket salon, with a maestro to shape her hair, to give her a new silhouette.

She asked her landladies, the sisters, for advice. They told her: 'I have heard the Rajputana has a spa. It's very good. Our cousin, she used to work there.' They sounded convinced. She took a taxi. As her handbag, her large leather batik handbag, slid through the security X-ray at the Rajputana, she felt an acute pang of memory, an anguished sense of separation from her canvas bag, from her manuscript, from *UNSUBMITTED*.

'Don't be silly, Rudrani,' she told herself, and walked resolutely into the magnificent interiors. It was still winter, even if it was Rajasthan, and yet the air-conditioning was set at a near-freezing level. Shivering, she tightened her new purple paisley shawl around herself and asked for directions to the spa.

One floor below lobby level a kind lady welcomed her at the salon reception. A middle-aged man with hennaed hair and a pencil moustache, also hennaed, made a fuss over her. He ruffled her hair this way and that, and examined her scalp as if he were a soil scientist.

'I will give you a new look, madam,' he announced. 'Even your best friends won't recognise you.'

Rudrani reflected, unsentimentally, that she had no best friends. No friends at all, really. Did Anirban count as a friend?

The stylist got to work, and there, before her eyes, her face emerged transformed, a new face, almost. The contours of her cheekbones, and her forehead, seemed sculpted afresh.

'You have beautiful skin, madam,' the man with the hennaed hair told her. 'And lovely hair, now we have worked on it.' The tag on his waistcoat read *Momin*. Just that: *Momin*.

He was done. She looked different and, she decided, better.

Momin was still fussing around her, pointing a mirror in different directions to show her how it looked from the various angles.

'I've given it a feather finish,' he told her.

She was fascinated by the word. 'A feather finish?' she asked. 'What's that?'

'I've layered it in a feather cut,' he explained.

She had been flipping through magazines while he worked on her hair. Now she pointed to a page in a fashion glossy. It had a beautiful woman, an older woman, with a cascade of purple hair.

'I want to look like that,' she said. 'Could you make me look like that?'

He looked her up and down in surprise. Then he looked at the magazine, studied it carefully.

TRENDS: Ombre purple-style craze, it said. He looked at the picture, and then at her, and laughed out loud in delight.

'Of course I will, madam,' he said. 'I like a challenge. There are several shades available: lilac, lavender, violet.'

'I love the colour purple,' Rudrani replied. 'Colour me purple, Mr Momin.'

He persuaded her to have a pedicure while he got to work. It took all of an hour, and the results were breathtaking. She was transformed. Transmuted. Metamorphosed.

Mr Momin had coloured the ends of her hair, of her feather-cut hair, and highlighted the rest. She examined herself with delight. She didn't look outlandish or grotesque, but stylish and daring. Like a witch in a comic cartoon. Like herself. 'You are a surprising lady, madam,' the hairdresser said admiringly. 'You have courage. Guts. Real *himmat.*' Gumption.

She didn't blink when she got the bill, and left him what was (by her standards) an extravagant tip. She swaggered out of the hotel and headed for the festival.

The lane leading to the Diggi Palace was full of people of different ages, nationalities and backgrounds, patiently making their way to the festival.

The pedicure and the haircut had energised her enormously. She walked along briskly, not dragging her feet as she usually did.

The Nobel laureate Vidhyadhar Shankardass was scheduled to speak in the Front Lawns. The writer for all seasons. Perhaps the greatest living writer of the age. She was determined to hear him and somehow managed to find a chair, just behind one of the poles that held up the tent, where she could get a partial look at him.

He was a frail benign figure, with gentle eyes that searched the crowds before him. He had to be helped up on to the stage, and he used walking aids, with grips, but with such grace that he didn't seem disabled at all.

His voice seemed to whisper into the microphone, and yet it could be heard with perfect clarity all the way to the last row, and beyond. 'I am an old man now,' he said, 'a wise old man at eighty-six. And I want to say this to all of you, readers, writers, book lovers. What is the point, what is the purpose, of so many books being written? The sheer weight of the output, of content creation and self-expression in these days of digital democracy, of all-accommodating platforms - I personally believe it devalues thought, devalues literature.'

The audience soaked it in. The beauty of his voice, the sense that he was confiding in them, sharing his thoughts with them.

Vidhyadhar Shankardass was in conversation with a famous editor and critic, who was evidently in great awe of him. 'I have to confide in you, and seek the indulgence of the audience,' the elderly man said now. 'I haven't really been listening to the questions, because I forgot to wear my hearing aids today. So I have been saying what I want, from my heart, and off the top of my head. And I will continue to do so. I hope you will hear me out.'

The audience broke out into cheers and whistles and thunderous applause.

Vidhyadhar Shankardass continued speaking, leading the audience through a master class on poetry, music and popular culture. There was a quality in his voice that made everyone listening in feel that he was reaching out to them alone.

Anura, the schoolgirl from the train, was taking in every word very carefully. He isn't old, she thought to herself. He isn't old at all. His mind is young. Perhaps as young as mine. From the corner of her eye, she was also observing the figure in the row ahead of her, two seats on the left of where she herself was sitting. It was an old woman with purple hair, cut in a short, chic style. She looked naggingly familiar, and yet not.

'Let us talk about the future,' the Nobel Laureate was saying now. 'People tell me that the future is now. The world - at least our world - is changing at an unprecedented pace. I will not live to see many of these changes, even those that are just around the corner, but many of you, my young friends in the audience, will witness them.'

His eyes scanned the audience. Anura felt that he was speaking only to her. 'Our stories will change too, as will the ways in which we tell them. The collective consciousness of the human race will find new resonance through the catalysts of artificial intelligence. I am no expert on technology, but I can feel this change, anticipate it, hear it in the whispers of the future.'

Anura felt a shiver run down her spine. This was her life, her future, that the Nobel Laureate was speaking about. She turned to her schoolfriend Farhan, seated next to her, and clutched his hand in excitement.

The woman in the row ahead with the purple hair stood up and began clapping. The audience shot in the screen beside the main stage zoomed in on her face, and Anura could see why she seemed familiar. She was the old woman in the train, the lady with the two bags, and their mysterious contents. She had cut her hair and coloured it purple.

It was strange, but not as strange, as wondrous, as Vidhyadhar Shankardass's vision of the future. She registered the inexplicable transformation of the old lady and then forgot about it, dismissing it as a minor mystery which didn't require investigation.

'To all our tomorrows,' the Nobel Laureate concluded, before the audience rose to accord him a thunderous standing ovation.

Anura and Farhan were to speak next at a session titled 'Imagine'. There were seven young speakers, each allotted seven minutes to hold forth on 'My Journey with Words'.

Anura was nervous. She had never really spoken in public before, while Farhan was a pro, an accomplished debater.

'Stay cool,' he counselled her. 'That's the rule. Stay cool.'

And she tried. But what unfolded that day changed something in her for ever.

It had begun well. A famous writer of Young Adult novels was moderating the session. She introduced the panellists with humour and generosity. A teenager who was an amateur astronomer began the session by reading from his novel about the mysteries of the universe. He concluded by quoting famous lines about astronomy being a humbling experience.

'And that is from *Pale Blue Dot: A Vision of the Human Future in Space*,' he concluded. 'By my hero, Carl Sagan.'

It took some time for the applause to die down. Farhan was next. He spoke of what writing meant to him and how, in his blogs, he valued truthfulness and a scrupulous respect for facts above all other things.

Nations and religions and tribes were only labels, he said: one had to be truthful to the human condition.

Suddenly, there was a scuffle in a corner of the tent, and a young rowdy hoisted himself up on a chair. 'Arre, you anti-national animal!' he screamed. 'Go back to Pakistan, you sickular!' He continued to shout, but the rest of his words were drowned in the din. Security came to pull him down, to take him away, but he had already toppled and fallen. He went down screaming, and there was a reflective silence as he was led out, even as the television cameras trailed his exit.

Farhan took the mic again and continued in a steady voice.

'I urge my friends in the audience to ignore this interruption,' he said, his voice suddenly sounding absurdly young, like the teenager he was, like a fifteen-year-old boy. Anura noticed that his hands were shaking.

'The speaker before me quoted from Carl Sagan,' Farhan continued, his voice still so steady that no one except Anura, who was seated on the stage and could see, would ever have realised that he was trembling. 'I too will quote him. "If a human disagrees with you, let him live. In a hundred billion galaxies, you will not find another." That is what I meant when I referred to the human condition.'

He continued until he had completed his seven minutes. The moderator had given him extra time to make up for the disruption.

There were other speakers after him. Anura was listed to talk last. She became aware that she was trembling, too, and that a hollow anger was building up inside her, like a rolling drum. She heard nothing, registered nothing.

When her turn came, she remembered only what Farhan had told her.

'Stay cool. That's the rule. Stay cool.'

She had no idea what she said for those seven minutes, but knew she delivered it well, fluently and convincingly. And then the anger took over again. And with the anger, love - a fierce, consuming love for Farhan.

She kissed him that evening, on the lips, and he moved back, alarmed. 'I don't think you should be doing that,' he said. 'You're only twelve.'

'And you are only fifteen,' she replied. 'And we are probably more grown up than most older people.'

They let it rest there, for the time being, and things went back to being as they had been. Almost as they had been.

Jaipur, January, Monday

Monday. The last day of the festival. The closing day when the weekenders have departed, for Mumbai, for Delhi, Chennai, Bengaluru, or begun their return to far-off spots across continents.

Rudrani had, in her past visits to the festival, enjoyed this last day the most. She would feel that the festival belonged to her, somehow, and to the other stragglers who had stayed behind.

However, this time she woke up on the Monday feeling tired, defeated and alone. The stitches hurt, and she felt woozy and disoriented. Even the presence of Dhola and Maru couldn't cheer her up. She put off returning Anirban's call, and debated the pros and cons of attending the festival in the state she was in.

I feel both exhilarated and empty, she wrote in her lined exercise book, under the heading Notes to Myself. *I need new experiences to fill me up, to replenish me.*

Her phone trilled, and it was Anirban again. 'You all right, lady?' he asked anxiously. 'We need to talk. Shall we meet at the festival, or should I come to see you?'

She didn't want him in her room, to see her like this. 'I will be there mid-afternoon, young man,' she said, 'waiting for you at the press terrace at three p.m. Sharp.'

She had recovered somewhat by noon, with the help of painkillers, tea and toast. It was a wrench to leave Dhola and Maru behind, but she could see the impracticality of taking them with her.

Three p.m. found her at the press terrace. Anirban arrived punctually too, accompanied by a strikingly handsome man, whom he introduced as a poet and translator.

'Juan has read your novel,' he explained, 'and he feels it can work for an international audience. He will be able to connect you with some people since he is an editor, and a scout, which means he helps a literary agency to locate new writers and books.'

She could feel her heart beating faster than it had ever done before. His words collided with the universe and echoed back, as though in a particle accelerator, or Moses receiving the tablets on Mount Sinai.

'What have you done to your hair, exactly?' Anirban asked cautiously. Rudrani didn't hear him, didn't reply to his question. Juan's words had left her speechless.

'This is just an instinct, a gut feeling, and you should not attach too much importance to it,' Juan cautioned, taking over. 'But yes, somewhere, somehow, this book will reach out and find readers.'

A spinster who lives alone cannot help but have a practical side, even if she is a novelist with a creative imagination.

'Let us get the paperwork straight,' Rudrani said, assuming control of the conversation. 'It's not money that I want, but recognition - of my book, of my story - not of myself.' She took out a large lined notebook from her capacious handbag. *TO WHOM IT MAY CONCERN* she wrote, in capitals with a purple gel pen, in her sloping handwriting. Then she returned to neat italic lowercase:

I, Rudrani Rana, aged 72 years and being of sound mind, hereby declare that I confer on Anirban M., whose signature is attached and attested below, the right to negotiate on my behalf for the publication of my novel The Face by the Window *(manuscript of 135,000 words), and to sign on my behalf on all matters related to this matter.*

She signed the letter with a flourish, and then handed it over to Anirban for his counter-signature.

'You can be the witness,' she told Juan. When he was done she rummaged in her handbag and took out her Aadhaar card. She wrote down her ID from her Aadhaar number, and her PAN card number as well, checking and rechecking them both meticulously.

'There you go,' she said. 'It's yours - do what you want with it. I may be travelling to Dehradun for a property case, but otherwise I will remain in Delhi. I know these things take time and I'm not expecting any miracles.'

They sat in silence for a few minutes.

'And about the hair,' Rudrani said, pointing at Anirban with her cane. 'It was simply a part of the process, of shedding, of moving on.' She began quoting from T. S. Eliot's 'Little Gidding'. 'For last year's words belong to last year's language, and ...' She got stuck there. 'Drat!' she said. 'My memory has given up on me. I'm shutting down, cell by cell.'

Anirban completed the lines for her. '...and next year's words await another voice.'

Juan was moved to the core. The old woman, her book, his new lover.

There was an incantatory feel to it, the three of them, amidst the crowds, having met by chance, and adhering together in so many deep and unexpected ways.

'I think there is a shift in the stars,' Rudrani said confidingly. 'There's this litigation, about some land my father's family owned, which has been going on for more than eighty years now. And suddenly it's looking as though it might - just might - get settled. A developer wants that land badly enough to pay everyone off.'

Anirban looked at the wrinkled figure with purple hair sitting before him, so full of hope and grit and endurance, and he felt a surge of affection for her.

'So it may happen,' she went on, 'if the stars align, that I shall become a rich woman. And then a famous one, if this book comes out, if the book succeeds.'

There was a wisp of coffee foam on her lips, a smear of chocolate éclair on her cheeks. 'There is a tide in the affairs of men/which, taken at the flood/leads on to fortune.' She quoted the lines with a hint of self-consciousness, then picked up her cane and her bag and rose unsteadily to her feet.

It was time for them to go their separate ways. Rudrani was tired, exhausted in fact, though she wouldn't admit it. She wanted to return to her room, put her feet up, take a double dose of painkillers and catch up with Dhola and Maru, who must surely be wondering where she was.

Anirban wanted to listen in to a session on 'A Sense of the Graphic: Hieroglyphics and Emojis!' And Juan had a Spanish friend speaking on '*Duende*: Mysteries of the Muse'.

'Would you like to come to the Writers Ball with us tonight, Lady Rudrani?' Anirban asked.

A creased smile lit up her face. 'But I'm not a real writer - not yet!' she replied. 'Let me see how I'm feeling after I get back to my lodgings. I take the afternoon train home to Delhi tomorrow.'

Anna Wilde hadn't spoken much in her session. It had been a crowded panel anyway, with too many people saying too few things. She had maintained what could be construed as an enigmatic silence. She had been circumspect about Allen Ginsberg, and his lover Peter Orlovsky. She had not mentioned her encounter with Robert Svoboda.

There were large chunks of memory she was still afraid to confront, unable to acknowledge. Anna felt as if she was floating in a dream, a dream trembling on the edge of a nightmare. This was not the India that she had known and loved, the mystic India that she had travelled the length and breadth of, that she had carried back with her in her heart to Colorado.

Her love affair with this chaotic country, with this transcendent culture, was still unresolved. Here she was in the same geography, with the same history, and yet it had transformed into another place. Times changed, people changed, and she herself had changed in the thirty years since she had last been here. But there had been a shift of perspective in this land where she had received her learnings.

The Summer of Love. Haight Ashbury, 1967. That was where this journey had begun, this passage to India. Tie-and-dye T-shirts and the smell of pot. The poetry had begun there, and the journeys, inwards and without.

America had changed. India had changed. Yet the song of India remained ageless inside her. It had entered like smoke and remained in her breath, in her vision, in what she was. She found herself humming the song called 'San Francisco (Be Sure To Wear Some Flowers in Your Hair)', a song she could have sworn she had forgotten, or at least not thought of for decades.

Where had they gone, all the gentle people?

Something of this festival reminded her of those times; it was a tug at memory. It was also a reminder of the fragility of those memories, of the circular passage of time, where everything was doomed to become the opposite of what it had once been.

The authors' lounge was strung with marigold flowers. It was a smell she associated with India, with Benares, with her then guru, and the burning ghats by which she had last met him.

She realised of course that it had always been a hocus pocus, an illusion, a game with herself. There were as many Indias as there were Indians, each with their own mysteries and paradoxes. Yet she felt betrayed, at the change, the boiling anger, the palpable tensions. When her travelogue *The Inner Eye* had first been published, she had described herself as 'a Hindu, a daughter of Mother India'. Well, now it was as though a wicked stepmother had taken over, she thought wryly.

So much of this festival had transported her back to that other India, that carnival of the mind. The Diggi Palace and its precincts evoked those ageless memories, which could nestle in its arches, until change came and swept them away.

Lost in her thoughts as she was, Anna Wilde looked down and saw that she had systematically shredded the petals off a garland of marigold flowers. They lay scattered around her in a fragrant, forlorn circle, to be swept away tomorrow.

It was the last day of the festival, and there was the sense of an ebbing tide, of dissipating energies.

Betaab was still processing the ideas he had been exposed to for the last few days. The man who lived in the 1 BHK flat in Noida, the silent master of daring heists, seemed now a distant memory.

It was poverty, and his father's cancer, that had driven him to theft. He had, skilfully and without compunction, taken what he needed from society. He had plucked the fruits he desired from the jungle of life. But what had driven him to poetry?

Betaab fretted over the metaphors of his thoughts. 'Plucking the fruits he desired from the jungle of life.' It sounded different in Urdu, but even then he was uneasy with it.

That is what a writer is, he thought to himself. A person who constructs and reconstructs his thoughts in order to understand what it is he is thinking, and then who shares them with the world in the most beautiful way possible.

This complicated explanation left him pleased, even satisfied.

'I was not born a burglar,' he told himself, 'but I was born a poet. And I will remain a poet.'

He was overcome by a sense of hope and resolve; he could see the path ahead as though on a Google map. It felt as if he was plotting a particularly audacious break-in. He drew a mental map, which included the geography and history of the target. Then he visualised entering it, and registered all the hurdles and obstacles he might meet.

Only now, today, it was not a dark, empty space he was entering. He shut his eyes and pictured where he would go, what he would do.

He saw himself, like the kite in his poem, soaring over the mustard fields, over the yellow desert sands. And then the blue ocean spread out before him; but he, his kite, did not falter. They flew effortlessly over the waves, and there before them was an unlimited expanse of sky and ocean.

And now he was a falcon, flying higher and higher, soaring where he pleased, while far below the earth was luminous and awaiting his return, as a mother her child.

He awoke from the reverie with tears in his eyes. Then his sensible self took over, planning, and plotting, strategising with ruthless and cold-blooded clarity.

As always, he imagined himself an interloper, an invisible disrupter of the expected. And there he was, breaking into Bollywood, on the throne of Bollywood, with his words, his voice, resonating in the hearts of all Indians. Lovers and anarchists, old married couples and schoolchildren, socialites and socialists, they would all cherish his songs, the poems he wrote, the dreams he shared.

Yes, he would steal their hearts, but he would not sell his dreams, or their dreams.

His mind reverted to common-sense everyday mode. He would get a small flat in Mumbai. Dada Sadarangani's mutual indebtedness club and his wide circle of contacts would help him set up base.

He would have to change his style. His previous profession had demanded extreme discretion, and he had been compelled to live beneath the radar, so to speak.

But to establish himself amidst the razzmatazz of the film world would demand savvy and style. He would need a mentor, or perhaps two, and connections, even though he was now a bestselling Urdu poet who had won an award at the Jaipur Festival.

But what if ...*what if he failed*? Suppose he didn't hit the jackpot as a film lyricist?

The prospect of once again facing the ignominy, the utter indignity of poverty, struck him like a physical blow. He could picture himself, in the 1BHK flat in Noida, surrounded by stacks of unsold books. He would meet Gunvanti Devi in the lift, and shed be as sad as him, perhaps even sadder. He would greet her politely and respectfully, and she would never know that he was the man who had robbed her of her wealth, and subsequently squandered it.

Betaab was so shaken up by the thought of a reversal of fortune that he slid to the ground and found himself hunched in the grass, oblivious to the crowds around him. He recalled his father in the tailoring shop, and the constant insults his customers had heaped upon him.

A sudden inspiration struck him, with all the force of a holy commandment. He would work upon one last burglary, build up a fortune of purple 2000-rupee notes, and enter Bollywood like a prince, a true *shehzada*.

It would be easy. The demonetisation effect had worn off, and the aggravations of the Goods and Services Tax had led to a new breed of GST evaders and facilitators. There were stacks of new notes, of unaccounted-for wealth, just crying to be spirited away. And, as he knew from past experience, these cash savings, hidden from the income tax net, when stolen were rarely reported to the police.

He got up and wandered off towards the tea stall, where fragrant masala chai was being ladled out into earthen cups. He had two cups, and then settled in a corner, taking in the scenes of the festival, all the time debating with himself the wisdom of returning to his old ways, if only for one last time.

He decided to take a round of the festival bookshop, to see if his books were still on display. The titles were arranged in alphabetical order, and his book was placed under 'B'. *Waqt Chor* by Razi Khan Singh 'Betaab', published by Alfaz Publications. There were still five copies on the shelf. It did not seem that they had managed to sell any so far.

Just then a commotion broke out at the rear of the tent. A spindly young man was being beaten up by the bookstore staff. A security guard was trying to intervene.

'They have nabbed a thief,' a bearded man was explaining to his wife. 'He tried to steal the safe-box with the day's takings. He crept in from the back, from under the tent, where the book cartons are stored.'

Two uniformed policemen had appeared. The thief was handcuffed and led out in disgrace, weeping, protesting his innocence.

Betaab felt a tug of sympathy for him. Things could go wrong for anyone, anywhere. But it was a shoddily planned job. The tented bookstore was too well lit, too crowded, for any chance of success. What could the fellow have been thinking?

He bought some books, and paid for them with his credit card. Poetry books. *Milk and Honey* by Rupi Kaur. She was on the closing session, generating hysteria among her fans. *Pluto* by Gulzar Saheb. A collection of Urdu poetry by Iftikhar Hussain, Javed Akhtar's grandfather, who wrote under the pen name of Muztar Khairabadi.

He stepped out to find a gaggle of agitated society ladies shouting at a security guard. Betaab had observed the type, the rich memsahibs with highlighted hair and expensive handbags which they always seemed to carry at a particular angle, though he had never actually met or spoken to one of the breed.

The memsahibs reminded him of the women, of a different social class admittedly, who had so regularly and so roundly abused his father for his lack of tailoring skills. An ancient resentment swelled in his heart. He hung around casually, to listen in to what the fuss was about.

One of their gang had 'forgotten' to pay for a book she had bought. The security guard had dared to apprehend her.

'Do you even know who I am?' she said to him, spitting out the words. 'I will have you chucked out of your job. I can have you arrested and put in jail, you stupid man!'

One of her friends had got her a glass of water to calm her down. The security guard handled her with practised ease.

'We can all make mistakes, madam-ji,' he said. 'I can, you can, we all can. I'm simply saying you forgot to pay for this book. So maybe you can go and pay for it now?'

His reasonable tone seemed to infuriate her even more. She had tears in her eyes, and her red-lipsticked mouth was contorted in an emotion that Betaab could not read. She hurled her heavy leather handbag and it hit the security guard square on the head.

Then she snatched the book from his hand and threw that back at him, too. 'You can keep the book, you *ulloo ka pattha*, you son of an owl,' she hissed. 'Though I don't suppose you know how to read, do you?' And she marched off self-righteously, followed by her friends.

The security guard shrugged his shoulders philosophically. 'The rich - they think they are different,' he observed, without bitterness. 'And they are. But they will surely have to pay the price for it someday.'

Betaab felt as though he had watched a morality play enact itself. Perhaps the cameo had been staged only for his benefit. He shook his head in puzzlement, still trying to decide whether to pull off one last heist before settling down to the pursuit of the poetic imagination.

He studied the programme. There were four sessions spread across different venues: a session by Rupi Kaur on the concept of Charbagh, the Four Gardens of Paradise as mentioned in the Qu'ran; another on 'The Politics of Language'. Three debut novelists were speaking on 'Last Words'. And there was to be an award ceremony for a French translation prize.

He felt weary of words, fatigued by all the conversation and discussion he had sampled during the last five days. He sensed that the world of letters, so beguiling from the vantage point of the outsider, of those wanting to break into the charmed circle, was in its inexorable process like any other, full of privileged hierarchies and lucky chances, of winning streaks and downward spirals of defeat and heartbreak.

He felt lost, and disconsolate, as he sat before the empty stage which was being readied for the closing debate. It was here, just two days ago, that he had recited his poem, won the prize for 'The Fallen Kite'. He had been transformed from a burglar into an artist. He had felt, like the kite in his poem, ready to soar the skies.

The betrayals of words were not like the betrayals of money. Money was currency, gold or bullion or cash, with promise to pay to the bearer the value of *x*. That was how he had thought of money, until that fateful day of 8 November, when money had become nothing, devalued to worthless paper on the whim of a prime minister.

Perhaps words were like that too, alluring and deceitful, their worth valid as long as the illusion of the game was upheld. They were symbols, and sounds - what did they have to do with the reality of substantial things or material life? They were only shadow creatures, invested with life by the minds of men.

He shook his head to shake off the weight of such complicated thoughts. He would make himself ill with words, he decided, if he was not careful.

Just then, the charming young volunteer who had informed him that he had won the poetry contest came up to him with an envelope in her hand. 'Greetings, Mr Betaab,' she said pleasantly. 'It's our closing event today and we wanted you to attend our Writers Ball tonight, if it's convenient for you. A bus will be leaving for the venue from the front gates at 7 p.m., and another at 7.15.'

A Writers Ball - who would have imagined it? He stared at the invitation in bemusement. Yes, he would go to the Writers Ball. He certainly would.

Rudrani Rana did not go to the Writers Ball, to which she was not in any case invited. She responded to Anirban's message by saying that she was too tired, that she needed to rest. She had been suffering from eye flashes again for the last few days, but ignoring them. She knew they were not dangerous. The eye doctor had explained it all to her.

'As the vitreous, the gel-like fluid that fills the inside of your eye, starts shrinking, it pulls on the retina, causing the retinal cells to fire off. It's not serious, and you don't have to worry; it's just a part of growing older.'

The flashing lights in her peripheral vision had always seemed, despite the doctor's perfectly rational explanation, some sort of message from heaven. To see lights, to hear voices - that was surely part of a writer's calling.

She took out a new notebook from her messy, much-rummaged-through suitcase and began writing. A writer couldn't stop. Ever.

Night Flashes: A Novel

She was sprawled on the bed, with the notebook before her. The Rajasthani puppets, Dhola and Maru, were seated in the only chair in the room, examining her curiously.

'I'm sorry,' she said, waving a finger admonishingly in their direction. 'I'm sorry, Dhola and Maru, but you are only puppets: it's me that's vested you with life. But now I'm going to get very busy again, with another story, a new story that has never been told before. So you will just have to be patient for a while, and stay silent while I get down to work.'

The bus was crowded, full of spent and exhausted authors. Betaab found himself seated next to a beautiful man with a mane of dark hair. He and Juan Torres got talking, and the Spaniard was delighted to find himself in the company of another poet.

'I am honoured to meet an Urdu poet!' he exclaimed. 'Too many of your countrymen write in the language of the conquistadors, and the English, she is a very bossy and aggressive lady. I cannot do without her, but I am not sure that I like her.'

The Writers Ball was noisy and carnivalesque, with all the colours and splendours of Rajasthan on show. The three of them sheltered in an alcove, fortified with excellent red wine.

Betaab was not really a drinker, although he sometimes drank Royal Salute or some other such IMFL (Indian

Made Foreign Liquor) whisky with his mentor, Dada Sadarangani. Johnnie Walker Double Black was his favourite 'imported' brand.

Juan Torres explained the mysteries of wine to him. 'Your Indian vino is excellent,' he said appreciatively. 'My namesake wine, Torres, has its denomination of origin in Penedes. It's the largest winery in Spain, and it has spread its roots to California, and Chile. But my favourite wine is quite different: she is the Rioja, the best wine in the world, born of the grape, Tempranillo. Drinking fine wine is like reading poetry; you have to understand the body of it, the structure, to enjoy it. Tell me more about your poetry,' he continued. 'Anirban, explain the poem, please. Read her for me in the English.'

Betaab showed Anirban the poem on his mobile and he read it intently, scrolling up and down to reread a line or a phrase. Then he got out his drawing pad, sketched a fallen kite on it, and wrote down the first verse in a free-flowing English translation. He read it out, slowly, with dramatic pauses and long silences.

Betaab was wonderstruck by the journey of words. 'Read it again, *bhai sahib*,' he pleaded, but Anirban had to make his way to the bar to replenish their glasses.

And then the second miracle happened. Juan began writing on the drawing pad, in a tiny neat script that looked like a garland of flowers. He read and reread his words a few times, then beamed triumphantly at Betaab.

'Your poem - she is now in the Spanish too,' he said. 'Listen.'

La Cometa Caida

Me remonte, recorri los cielos.
En tus manos firmes
me deje llevar por el viento,
volando como un halcon,
cruzando campos de mostaza en flor
y las arenas amarillas del desierto,
hasta que el oleaje azul del oceano
si hizo mi dueno
Ya ti? Donde es que to deje atras?

Anirban returned holding two overflowing glasses of wine which he redistributed into three equal portions.

Juan read out the poem again, so Anirban could appreciate it.

'This poem, she has *duende*,' Juan explained. 'You will doubtless ask me, what is this *duende*? Let me tell you the story from within. *Duende* is the most secret Spanish word. Nowadays people use it this way and that, without thinking, without consideration. But I will explain it to you in the language of Lorca, of Federico Garcia Lorca in his essay "La teoria del duende". *Duende* is a mysterious force that no philosopher can explain. It is the pain within us, the wounding, and also the healing.'

The wine, Anirban's translation into English, and now hearing his poem in Spanish, Betaab felt he was on a different plane altogether, far, far removed from the human dimension of his other existence. For some reason, Gunvanti Devi's face appeared before him like an apparition; her face as he had seen it the last time he had met her in the lift, in Noida. Tears rose unbidden to his eyes, why and for whom or what he did not know.

'*Duende* - how do I say it in another language?' Juan was on a roll. 'An old maestro of the guitar, he has said, "The *duende* is not in the throat; the *duende* rises up from inside of you, from the soles of the feet".'

They toasted the spirit of *duende* and went off in search of some food.

Gayatri was at the Writers Ball too. She had come with Sumedh; they were both lost in each other, as though they had drunk of some murky love potion. Carmen of the auburn hair had left for Kerala, for a fortnight at an Ayurvedic spa, convinced that it was she who was abandoning Sumedh, completely innocent of his perfidy.

The Bollywood band was playing nostalgia numbers from the sixties and the seventies. Sumedh Kumar and Gayatri were jiving enthusiastically to the strains of 'Dum Maro Dum'. She was dressed in the pale pink sari with the silver border, the one Anirban had described as *pyaazi*, as onion pink.

She felt every bit as beautiful as Zeenat Aman in the film - young, uninhibited, rebellious. She had found love, or love had found her.

They had both completely abandoned themselves to the music, and were making the most funky and uninhibited moves. Writers are not always the best dancers, but even the most intense, bearded, pedagogical and intellectual of the speakers had entered into the spirit of the dance. They moved their weight from foot to foot and lip-synched the words from 'Hare Krishna Hare Rama', waving their hands stiffly in different directions as they did so.

Gayatri was the belle of the ball. She shook her hips, undulated her torso, wiggled her boobs, waved her arms, tapped her feet. Sumedh Kumar tried valiantly to keep pace with her, but she was so lost in the music, so swept away by the euphoria of the moment, that he appeared clumsy and diffident before her.

Anirban M. and Juan Torres cut in and joined her on the floor.

Sumedh Kumar exited towards the restroom, then settled down resignedly on a cane chair, a spectator once more. He wondered where Carmen was, and why she had departed, leaving just a cryptic line in explanation.

See you later, stranger, she had written in the note addressed to him that the boy at the hotel reception handed over. He had tried to call but her phone remained switched off. Was she on a long flight? Flying off where? To whom?

He should never have left Gayatri in the first place, all those years ago. He felt safe and secure to be back with her. There was something about one's early loves. She knew the Sumedh he had been, and still to some extent was - not just the American professor with confused loyalties and an increasing distance between the here and there of his life.

And she looked good, very good, in a sari. The pale pink suited her, and the dangling silver earrings added an allure to her face. Yes, he had done the right thing. *They* had done the right thing. Things would sort themselves out, somehow.

He had a crick in his back from dancing too much. But Gayatri looked happy, and he was content with that.

Gayatri was happy for many reasons. She was happy because she had got Sumedh Kumar back; he had been returned to her, by some divine karmic forces she could still not completely understand.

She was also happy, and immensely relieved to have thrown her manuscript away. She had walked at dusk by the embankment of Man Sagar Lake. Her manuscript - the 27,000 words of *The Heart Has Its Reasons* that she had slaved and sweated over for the last two years - had been wrapped in a brown paper cover, with a garland of marigold flowers tied around it.

She had bought the bright orange garland from a woman who was selling flowers outside a small temple, a shrine with marble statues of Lord Krishna and the mistress of his heart, Radha Rani.

Radha was not Lord Krishna's wife. He was married to the Lady Rukmani, and also, if Gayatri remembered aright, to Satyabhama. He had also married the 16,100 women prisoners whom the demon Narakasura held captive. Oh well.

Gayatri had knelt down and prostrated herself before the divine milkmaid, Radha Rani, and her lover, the cowherd-god Krishna. She had slipped a 100-rupee note into the donation box. Then she had wrapped her double-spaced spiral-bound manuscript in the strings of marigold and walked alongside the lake. The sunset was the colour of the marigold flowers. She had hurled the packet into the water, where it had landed with a soft plop.

'I want to live love, not write about it,' she had told herself. She couldn't recall whether she had spoken the words out loud, or said them softly to herself in her thoughts.

The Heart Has Its Reasons, all the carefully thought-out phrases, the commas and pauses, the corrected spellings, the thesaurus consultations, the unities of plot and character, of time and action, were thrown into the waters of the man-made Man Sagar Lake. It was a symbolic gesture, an affirmation of intent, a return to herself.

'Life, not words,' she said again, out loud this time. The shadows had crept in. The marigold flowers had settled in the shallow water; the crimson and orange of the sunset had departed the sky.

The spiral-bound manuscript would dissolve and disintegrate. The ink would become one with the water. The paper would become pulp. Only the plastic spiral binding would remain, its skeletal presence like the vestige of some ancient marine life.

It was when she was walking back, looking for an auto-rickshaw, that the memory of Carlson rose in her heart. Her husband who had not been her husband. The past that was not the present. She sighed. She had thrown all the old narratives away. Here and now, a new future awaited.

But was it just the comfort of habit that had drawn her back to Sumedh? she fretted. The habit of being hurt?

Would she ever have the courage - or the conviction - to discard that narrative?

Perhaps someday. But not today. Not today.

Back at the Writers Ball, the merriment continued. The band moved to Bollywood songs from the eighties. Gayatri was still dancing, sashaying and shimmering in her onion-pink sari. Her pallav had slipped off her shoulders, exposing the skimpy sequinned blouse below.

Sumedh came up to her. He looked troubled, even unhappy, as he whispered something unintelligible into her ears. She could smell the onions and kebabs on his breath, but she couldn't make out what he was saying.

He pulled her aside. 'Your blouse,' he muttered. 'It's too tight, too small, and your boobs are spilling all over the place.' He draped the sari pallav proprietarily around her shoulders and gave her a kiss on her cheek.

Gayatri stared at him in astonishment. Then she winked. 'My blouse, my boobs,' she said cheerily, as she returned to the dance floor.

Later, after the dance was over, she pondered his discomfort with her skin, and her own new-found comfort with it. Something in the pattern was not right, she could see that it was not.

'I'll just have to learn to manage him,' she shrugged to herself. 'Or else ...'

Meanwhile, Betaab had gone up to the stage and seized the mic. It screeched in his inexpert hands, and then there was silence, or relative silence; no music, but the murmuring of excited voices, laughter, the chink of glasses and cutlery.

'A mic is a transducer that employs air-pressure variations to convert sound waves to an electrical signal,' Juan Torres told Anirban M.

It sounded profound, and philosophical, like a poem almost. Anirban looked at his Spanish friend in adoration. '*Te quiero, Juan*,' he said. 'I love you, Juan.' He was careful to pronounce the Spanish words right. Not for nothing had he practised them before his bathroom mirror, with an audio-check from his iPad.

Betaab had control of the mic now, and was singing softly and confidently.

It was a ghazal, by Faiz Ahmad Faiz. He had always disdained Faiz Saheb's revolutionary poetry, but here he was, singing it with belief and passion.

'Speak, your words are yet free - speak, for your voice is still your own.'

He forgot the lines halfway, bowed and got off the stage to thunderous applause. Other writers took over, singing with different degrees of talent in tongues and languages not everyone could understand.

And Zoya Mankotia? She had read and reread Rudrani Rana's poison-pen missive every day, indeed several times a day, since she had received it. It had stung her afresh, deeper and with greater force, each time. She had almost begun to get used to the pain, to the sweet solace of those hurtful words.

According to Plutarch, Cleopatra had chosen the deadly poison of the asp as her chosen path to death, had embraced the venomous Egyptian cobra and welcomed its sting.

'It's just a jealous, perverted mind at work,' her friends had consoled her. 'A frustrated writer, an antediluvian troll.' But the words had rung true, somewhere, and she had been unable to let them go.

Zoya Mankotia didn't go to the Writers Ball. She stayed in her room, and settled herself on the tiny balcony, a bottle of Jack Daniel's whiskey beside her and a bottle of soda kept discreetly on the tiled floor - it would cool soon in the desert night. A bucket of ice on the plastic table.

There were magnificent fireworks exploding in the sky as an extravagant wedding procession made its way somewhere in the lanes below. The octagonal balcony made her feel suspended in a module of timeless space. It was like being in an empty airport lounge, or in a Tokyo capsule pod hotel room, with the night sky as her psychedelic flat screen.

The letter. She took it out from her handbag, where she had kept it safe in a plastic folder. It was too dark to read it clearly, and the dim light on the stone wall let out only a minimal gleam.

But there was no need to reread it. She had committed it to memory. Engraved it in her heart.

'Miaow, miaow, Ms Mankotia! I can see through you. You faithless bich, I know what you have been up to, how many women you have betrayed. What's more, your pathetic intellectual pretenshuns leave me speechless! And your novel, *The Quilt*, is a copycat version of Ismat Chughtai's *Lihaf*. You plagiarizer, you pornographer ... Your time is up.'

Two stiff shots of Jack Daniel's - she hadn't bothered with the soda - had cleared her brain. She went over the letter, point by purple point. From the bottom up, this time.

Her time was *not* up. She was in the prime of life, in good health, of sound finances, respected and appreciated in some quarters. The homophobes and lesbian-haters and right-wingers and ultra- conservatives might hate her, but that was that. Their time was up, not hers.

It was two years ago that she and her wife had been attacked. Off-campus accommodation, small-town America. The new America. They had been in bed together, making love, an after-dinner cuddle, really, when the men had broken in. They had masks on their faces. Whips in their hands. Her wife had climbed on top of Zoya to protect her. To take the blows on her behalf.

One of the men had kicked her in the face with a booted foot. He had fractured her nose. There was blood on his boots. Blood on the bed, her hair, their faces. Blood everywhere.

The men had sprayed the word CUNTZ on the front door, all in capitals. It didn't sound like a swear word, feel like an insult.

The men were apprehended and detained by the police. One of them admitted to the assault. He did his time in jail. The other two were acquitted.

PIGZ. Homophobic pigs. Their time was up.

The Quilt. It was *not* plagiarised. It was inspired by her wife, Rowena, her loyal wife, her courageous wife, who had climbed over her to take the blows.

Of course she had read Ismat Chughtai. But her story had nothing to do with Chughtai, with *Lihaf*. So why did the words still hurt?

'Your pathetic intellectual pretenshuns leave me speechless.' The deliberate misspelling was surely a 'pretenshun'. No, that was not where it hurt. That was only unfunny.

'I can see through you. You faithless bich, I know what you have been up to, how many women you have betrayed.'

Yes, she had been a faithless bitch, a philandering bitch. It was a polyamorous world, and each act of love only added to the sum of the total. She loved, she was loved. What was wrong with that?

The purple pen did not - could not - know what she had suffered. Only she could deconstruct the narrative of her life. The self-loathing. The words that had been said. The things that had been done. The scars that remained.

The damage done. A little bit of it in everyone. And then we try to erase it, she thought, to wipe it clean. But the spots remain, the stains; and the love within, it curdles, turns to poison.

Rowena had tried to kill herself when she found out. She survived, and they loved each other again; perhaps Rowena loved Zoya even more than before.

But the dark worm had found its way inside again. After four whiskies it almost didn't hurt to remember. She wondered if it was too late to go to the Writers Ball. Then decided that yes, it was indeed too late.

Deep below the comfort of the whiskey, the letter rankled still. It was a fork in the road, a turning point. Or was it?

But it was not too late to forgive herself. There was still time for that, and a way to do it. She would write a letter to herself, in purple ink. A self-addressed letter, stamped in the post office of Nowhere. Return to Sender. A poison-pen missive - a sequel, perhaps, to *The Quilt*.

Another whiskey downed and she fell asleep, there on the balcony, in the not-so-comfortable chair. She awoke shivering. It was still dark. The night was very silent. A troubled light shone from behind the gathering clouds.

She went back inside and ate a bar of chocolate. Brushed her teeth and got into bed, between the covers. Got up again and read, for the last time, the pussycat card with the message in purple ink. Then she tore it up and threw it into the dustbin, where it lay next to the curled-up wrapper from the chocolate bar. She fell asleep, and awoke with only the lightest of hangovers.

The festival was over. Now for the connecting flight, and then the flight back. Zoya was a tidy packer, and she hadn't really messed up her bags at all. She went through the drawers, threw away the pointless goodies, the gift books, the stationery, the bookmarks, in the delegate bag. She kept the Ayurvedic hand lotion, and the small silver lamp, stuffing them into the side zip of the smaller bag.

She was making notes in her head, as writers do. On second thoughts, she emptied out the cane waste basket, now full of all the bumf she had discarded. She reached to the very bottom, where the torn-up pussycat card nestled beside a sticky chocolate wrapper. Picked up the pieces, now smeared with chocolate, which she wiped away carefully. Put them away in a brown paper envelope, as though she was a policeman, or a detective, filing away some important forensic evidence.

Zoya Mankotia got dressed for the flight, donned her black velvet tracksuit and silver sneakers. 'Screw it,' she said to herself. 'I am who I am.' She reassembled her face, smiled at herself in the mirror, and stepped out of the room, shutting the door behind her.

After Stories

Anna Wilde, Benares, February

Quentin Cripps and Anna Wilde: two figures silhouetted by the banks of the river, in Assi Ghat. They had met in the Harmony Bookshop, and recognised each other from the festival.

Quentin had asked at the bookshop if they had copies of *Disney and the American Dream*. They didn't, but the owner promised to order some copies, and noted his name.

'Are you a descendant of Stafford Cripps?' the man asked him.

'No …should I be?' he had replied.

And there was Anna Wilde: he had heard her at the festival. The owner, Rakesh, seemed to know her, and greeted her enthusiastically. Yes, he had copies of *The Third Way* and *The Inner Eye* - he had made sure they were in stock.

There were rumours of a lynching, of an impending curfew. Rakesh urged the couple to return to their hotels. But they disregarded him, tarrying by the ghats, by the holy river.

There was a chemistry between them, the sort of instant friendship that strikes up between strangers and fellow travellers, especially when they are in strange lands. Anna found Quentin profoundly naive and felt protective on that count. Quentin felt as though he was inside the frame of a postcard, an exotic picture of eternal India with every cliché in the book, sparing none.

'So what were the sixties like?' he asked her, a note of wonderment in his eyes, as though he were preparing to listen to a fairy tale.

'They say, "If you remember the sixties, you weren't really there",' she replied, straight-faced.

'And what do you make of this?' he persisted, waving his hands against the setting sun.

'Of what?' she asked.

'India - this place ...'

Anna looked around her. She felt completely at home, as though she had never left. The texture of the air, the smell of the river, welcoming her with gentle reproach for being away for so long.

'I came as a pilgrim,' she replied, 'as a pilgrim and a student. I learned Sanskrit here, at the Benares Hindu University. From my guru, I learned to suspend judgement. I learned to eat spicy food, and to be careful about the water I drank. I learned to unlearn my learnings, and that was the greatest gift this city gave to me.'

'So tell me your story,' he said, 'and your learnings.'

She was silent for a while. The sun was setting, and the river turning grey. He observed how beautiful she was, how supple and strong.

She remembered a story she had read, from the Indian scriptures. It had made a deep impression on her when she first encountered it.

*

The sage Narada had asked Lord Vishnu the meaning of Maya and the nature of delusion. The Lord had led the sage to a pool. 'Let us take a dip in these waters,' he said, 'and partake in the ritual of purification.'

When they were knee-deep in the pond, surrounded by pink water lilies and humming bees, Vishnu transformed Narada into a beautiful woman. As she stepped out of the pond, her eyes met those of a handsome man dressed in fine robes. He led her to his carriage, and she travelled with him to a nearby fort. He was a powerful king, a wise and generous ruler, and he begged her to marry him. She became the chief of his queens and bore him four sons and three daughters. The kingdom prospered, until it was attacked by a neighbouring ruler. A bitter war erupted. Three of her four sons died in battle. The fourth son fell from his horse and died while returning victorious from the field. Even as she was nursing her grief, there was a cloudburst and the city was flooded. The rising waters reached the high ramparts of the fort and swept everything away. Her husband, her daughters, all were drowned.

She was weeping and bewailing her fate when she heard a voice. 'Narada! O Narada! Why are you still standing in the pond? You have been there for half an hour now.'

Lord Vishnu had appeared to remind her of the powers of Maya and the nature of delusion. Narada returned to his earlier form, but carried the understanding of the ephemeral nature of his dream-self with him through all his days and incarnations.

★

Anna decided not to tell Quentin the story. It was too complicated and required too many explanations. But her own story floated and rose to the surface, as though the waters of forgetfulness had been cleared from her heart and her mind's eye.

Anna Wilde. Born Annika Wilderton. The only child of only children. She had set upon writing a trilogy when she was fifteen, which was when she became Anna Wilde. The trilogy was on the theme of Time, and remained uncompleted, but after that her birth name and pen name fused and became one, shedding the two vowels and four consonants that had tied her to her former self.

Anna Wilde wrote a play when she was twenty-two, about a man who got lost inside himself. It was published under her new pen name, IK Nsen. Her mother, who was convinced of her daughter's poetic destiny, had the play published and bound, though it was never staged, except once as street theatre in Paris, in 1968. Anna had a boyfriend who translated it into French, and they had to struggle through many explanations and anagrams and diagrams before she could finally make him understand how Annika Wilderton, Anna Wilde and IK Nsen were in varying degrees the same person.

That summer in Paris had led Anna to India; she had come to study at the Sorbonne for her junior year abroad, and found herself in a city of barricades and protest songs, of long-haired students in flared trousers and an urban war that carried within it the sweet smell of love.

The Sorbonne had been declared a people's university. *Il est interdit d'interdire*. It is forbidden to forbid. This became a famous slogan in May 1968. Was this liberation? Was this anarchy? Nothing could go on as it had before May 1968, and it did not.

France returned from the brink. Anna Wilde broke up with her boyfriend. Annika Wilderton continued to receive an allowance from her mother. IK Nsen continued to paint vibrant colours with rough strokes on canvas. In the middle of all this she saw Jean Renoir's classic film, *The River*, and then nothing was ever the same again. From the very first opening shots, of a circle being drawn in rice paste on a mud floor, she felt an immense sense of recognition, of belonging. 'For those of you asking for something new and different in entertainment - India in Technicolour. *The River.*' Only this was not entertainment. This was, had been, would be, her life. She watched the film in the theatre three times, back to back, and knew she had to go to India, to be by the banks of the Ganges, and find herself.

Anna landed in New Delhi on Thursday 4 July by Air India. The return ticket was valid for a year. It was hotter than anybody could have ever imagined. She lay in her ground-floor room in the YWCA, stripped of all her clothes, watching the ceiling fan as it circulated the hot breath of the room in futile circles. She had no idea what she would do next.

That evening, she visited the Monkey temple, a short walk away from the YWCA. It was crowded and dirty and fragrant, and she felt suddenly at home and at ease. There were bangle-sellers and flower-sellers and sweet shops and women squatting on the ground applying henna to other women who sat on low stools holding out their palms. Anna was so enchanted that she quite forgot about the heat. She got talking with a group of Americans who seemed to know their way around. They were going to the mountains the next day, to visit an ashram they had heard about.

'Want to join us?' one of them asked her. 'It will be cooler than here. It will be raining, though, as the monsoon will have set in.'

Anna had no idea what a monsoon was, but she nodded. 'Yes, I'll join you,' she said decidedly. And that was that.

'If you remember the sixties, you weren't really there.' That's what they said, only partly in jest. One was supposed to be just too stoned to remember anything. She had been clear-eyed when she reached the mountains, after a journey in a bumpy bus that felt like a ship in rough weather. It was raining in the last stretch and water streamed in through the windows.

She barely knew her new friends, and yet they were bathed in a sort of communal trust, a tribal intimacy. They took a ramshackle taxi for the last stretch, and then they were there, at the Kainchi Ashram, in the Himalayas. Their surroundings were shrouded in mist and fog, and a light but determined drizzle beat down on them. There was a sort of sweetness in the air - she couldn't put her finger on it but there it was, like ozone, or a good trip.

They were led into a long, low room, lit with kerosene stoves. Electric bulbs dangled from the wooden rafters, but they did not throw any light. Two young white men, possibly Americans from their accents, were playing on what seemed to be portable organs. Their fingers caressed the black and white keys, and they crooned a mantra she could partially decipher. Hare Rama, Hare Krishna, Krishna Krishna, Hare Hare. Allen Ginsberg had chanted the mantra, as had George Harrison. But not like this, with rain beating on a tin roof, and the smell of incense in the air.

The Beatles had visited an ashram at Rishikesh that spring, and the papers had been full of it. Anna felt as though she had wandered into a collective dream. She also realised that she was very, very hungry, that she hadn't eaten for what might be days. Bananas materialised before her, and warm milk in a copper tumbler, and she was led off to a rope bed with a dry mattress and a woollen blanket before she passed out.

She woke up in the dark before the dawn and stepped outside. She was surrounded by stars, swimming in them. The Milky Way snaked through the sky, and then, before her dazzled eyes, a meteor shower streaked and illuminated the tapestry above. Somewhere, not from the sky above, but somewhere around her, like a whisper, she heard her mother's voice. 'Annika, are you all right? Annika, are you all right?'

The voice caught at her heart. 'I'm all right, Mother,' she replied. 'I'm missing you.'

'I'm missing you too, Annika,' her mother said. 'Call me, please. I think I'm going away.'

Then the breeze, whistling through the pines. A lantern, and two women emerged from a doorway. They were draped in white saris, and moving with the quiet placidity of set routine. They walked downhill, towards the sounds of the river. She could hear the water, hurtling through the rocks and boulders. She followed them, straining to hear her mother's voice again, in the breeze, in the water. But there was nothing.

They placed the lantern on a rock and made their way to the water. She saw them silhouetted in the dim light, scooping up the water, then returning it with cupped hands to the flowing river. Suddenly there was birdsong in the air. Dawn was breaking in the sky.

Anna followed them back. 'Excuse me,' she asked them. 'I need to call my mother in America. How do I do that, please?'

The younger of the two, a radiant middle-aged woman with an aura of deep calm around her, took charge. She summoned a tall man draped in a blanket and instructed him to take Anna to the PTO in Nainital. 'The Post and Telegraph Office,' she explained. 'You can place a collect call from there. Tell the postmaster, Mr Shah, that Ma has sent you.'

She untied a little knot at the edge of her sari and took out some money. 'You may need this,' she said. 'Remember, we are your mothers too. Have some tea before you leave.'

A shared taxi. Nainital. A green lake. A bazaar. The Post and Telegraph Office. The postmaster, Mr Shah. She placed a collect call to her aunt, her mother's sister, in New York.

It took an hour for the operator to patch the call through. 'It's me, Anna,' she said. 'I'm worried about Mother. I thought I heard her calling me.'

It was late at night in NY. Her aunt was sobbing at the other end. 'Annika!' she said. 'Annika, how did you know? She had a fall yesterday. She is asking for you.'

Anna never returned to the ashram. She took a bus to New Delhi, a taxi to the airport. Forty-eight hours later she was in the hospital, with her mother. She remained with her, all that year, until she died. Then Anna returned to India again.

The next time around was different. She had returned in another mood, hit another trail. She had come here, to Benares, and written her first book, *The Third Eye*.

She sat here now, in Benares, remembering those days. In 1997, less than a week before he died, the terminally ill Allen Ginsberg had written a poem, 'Things I'll Not Do (Nostalgias)'. When she had first read the poem, she had promised herself that she, Anna Wilde, would never likewise be drawn in by nostalgia, never return to those ancient haunts to seek out the past.

But the invitation to the literature festival had been too tempting to refuse, and then it seemed perverse not to make the pilgrimage to the site of her dreams and nightmares. It had taken years of meditative practice to heal the traumas of those years, and to restore herself to the person she now was. She could be here now, in the fullness of the present, the stronger for the tests and trials she had endured.

Anna had been drawn into the web of esoteric tantric practices with her then boyfriend. Their guru had named her Vajrayogini. The boyfriend had eventually returned to study the relative certainties of physics, while Vajrayogini stayed back to unravel the shadowed mysteries of the path with the guru.

Her guru had instructed her that the first steps in dismantling the ego would be painful and bewildering. She could sense herself falling apart, as every certainty collapsed around her.

She had become obsessed with death. She would sit for hours by the ghats, watching the flames, breathing in the sweet-acrid stench of ghee and burning flesh and damp wood. When she returned to the ashram, the sex too was savage-sweet. It was not sex, her guru insisted, but initiation. 'The path to life lies through death,' he explained, 'and the path to death is only through the satiation of the flesh.'

'The man is a bully and a sadist,' her other self, the observer IK Nsen, would note, in an entirely clinical fashion. 'Anna Wilde has succumbed to the onslaught of nonsense. When will she wake up?'

One day, Anna Wilde walked out of the ashram, and away from her guru, taking Annika Wilderton, IK Nsen and Vajrayogini with her.

She went to a barber and had her ragged shoulder-length blonde hair shaved off. She decided to spend a month in Rishikesh, and travelled upriver to write her heart out. *The Third Way* emerged from many voices, from the fierce learnings of Vajrayogini, the wonder and curiosity that had consumed Annika Wilderton, the wry wisdom of IK Nsen.

She sent the manuscript off to a well-known academic press and it was published soon after she returned to the

States. She never returned to India again, not until now. It was only Anna Wilde who sat by the holy river today, though she carried all those other fragments of herself somewhere within, as a cat might its contented kittens.

Her story. Anna Wilde's story. Annika Wilderton's story. IK Nsen's story. Vajrayogini's story. She was not going to share it. It was like all the other stories in the world: a dream within a dream.

'My guru ...he let me down,' she said reflectively. 'People do it all the time, but he was my guru. He didn't acknowledge the boundaries between me and himself. He claimed that in fact there were no boundaries between him and the universe. Guru-ji used to say that wisdom would hit me on the head - plonk! - like a coconut falling from a tall palm. Well, it did. My mother, she was special. She taught me to respect myself. But Guru-ji had broken me down to my parts, deconstructed me. Perhaps I was a bad disciple, perhaps I lacked the discipline, but I left.'

Anna Wilde straightened her back, closed her eyes and breathed deeply. Quentin watched her, and observed the silence that encircled her amidst the hooting traffic, the cries of street vendors, the tolling bells, the castanets, the sounds of prayer.

She awoke from her meditations and smiled. 'So what's your story, Quentin?' she asked.

'My story?' he replied. 'It's one of the oldest stories in the world. I lost my woman. She walked out on me. I loved her too much. I tried too hard. That's all.'

She looked at him, and it was as though he could see the river flowing in her eyes.

'You will heal,' she said. 'You will mend. It took me some time to reassemble myself, but I mended into something better than I had been. I had learnt something about my ego, and myself, and my atman. Paradoxically, Guru-ji was the coconut that hit me on the head.'

She paused. The smell of incense, the sounds of prayer wafting across the waves.

'He taught me a lot, my guru. I wish I had been able to teach him something in return.'

'That sounds like a parable,' Quentin said. 'Perhaps I should make you my guru.'

They set off to explore the city and its stories.

Betaab, somewhere, March

Betaab was balanced on the very edge of the terrace. The security guards hadn't glimpsed him, and he had strategically evaded the CCTV cameras, which were placed in all the expected, predictable vantage points. He felt he was levitating a few inches above the ground, in a trancelike state of meditation. He could smell the spill of diesel oil near the generator set. There was a fragrance of floral detergent, where clothes had been dried. He knew that the terrace was empty, and that there was an open door flapping slightly in the breeze which led through the stairwell to the floor below.

The door leading to the fourth-floor flat was locked, but he would easily manage that. He was carrying two long, delicate iron files, a blade, a special magnet and a silver fork with sawn-off spikes in an innocuous-looking plastic bag that said *Krishna Tailors, Beadonpura*. He had a superstitious attachment to the bag; it had always been lucky for him and he carried it on such excursions like a mascot.

Betaab wore expensive sports shoes which had been carefully weathered to look old, worn and unremarkable, with Gucci ankle-length casual socks which he had ordered online. He was superstitious about that too. They had to be blue, or grey, never black. Underneath were two sharp blades, wrapped in thick double foil. He could feel the blades under the soles of his feet; they kept him grounded, alert to danger.

He flexed and unflexed his toes to relax and maintain his concentration. Then he crawled at floor level towards the door, soundlessly, like a fish swimming in water. The door creaked, the joints were rusty, but whoever might be listening would be used to that.

A dog barked. A man laughed. '*Saala kutta*,' he said. 'That idiot dog will never stop yelping.' A woman giggled, and whispered something in reply. Servants. Fucking servants, making out in the terrace. Servants fucking.

The calm confidence that had enveloped him was shaken.

'*Arre, chumbi de de*,' the man's voice wheedled. Give me a kiss. The woman giggled again.

A spurt of anger rose within Betaab, like a flame. Then it subsided into irritation. He had never lost his composure before, on a job. This was the first time, and it was not a good sign.

He tried to visualise what was happening. A man and a woman, hiding from the sahibs. They did not want to be discovered.

There was a generator set near the door, with a space behind it which was a sort of natural cubbyhole. He had scoped it all out two days ago. He crawled towards the generator, then coughed. A loud, assertive cough.

They heard him. 'Shhh,' the man said, then there was complete silence.

Betaab stayed hidden behind the generator set for six minutes, timing it with his breathing. Then he made his way down the stairwell. There was a hidden camera on the landing, but he had already worked out how to circumvent it. An unidentifiable figure might show up on the peripheral vision, but nothing beyond that.

The lock was a beauty. The expensive ones were, if anything, easier to unscramble. A half sawn-off fork, a flick of the wrist, and another on the double-cylinder deadbolt. He was speaking to the lock, singing to it, and it was responding.

Inside the flat, the fragrance of Rajnigandha: fresh tuberoses. An empty house with fresh flowers? Something was wrong. The flat belonged to a wealthy film distributor who had gone to Vienna for a holiday with his wife. His daughter lived in Mumbai. So who was in the flat?

Betaab was carrying his phone in his pocket - something he normally never did. He flashed the phone torch around, shielding it with his gloved fingers. The velvet sofa was strewn with multi-coloured cushions. A table, piled with books and papers. An iPad.

He knelt down to look at the books. Gulzar. Javed Akhtar. Faiz Ahmed Faiz. In Urdu. In Devanagari. In Roman English. The books were marked and annotated. A pad of yellow notepaper had what looked like a film script and storyboard.

His two lives had collided. Was there a writer in the flat? Perhaps the daughter from Mumbai?

What was he doing here? What was the poet Betaab doing in a fourth-floor flat, trying to rob a film distributor who was holidaying in Vienna with his wife?

He knew the locker would be in the prayer room. It would be concealed behind the small mandir with the shrine to Lakshmi.

To whom did he owe allegiance: to Lakshmi or Saraswati? The Goddess of Wisdom or the Goddess of Wealth? Who was he - Raju or Betaab?

The answer rose from within him. He was a poet. Not a thief.

But he decided to check out the locker all the same. He couldn't leave halfway after breaking in, could he?

The prayer room contained an overpowering smell of stale incense. A lamp with an electronic flame glimmered inside. Pictures of gods and goddesses covered the walls.

The wooden panelling with brass inlay opened into a small cupboard which revealed an old-fashioned steel locker. Betaab extracted the neodymium magnet, which was placed inside a tattered sock. He played with it, probing the steel surface of the locker, stroking and tapping it as he tried to locate the vulnerable spot where the nickel heart was located.

It opened almost immediately. Betaab beamed the light from his mobile phone and ferreted out the contents. A pouchful of emeralds. Wads of 100-dollar bills: at least 20,000 dollars, he estimated. No rupees, no post-demonetisation purple notes.

He was suddenly bored with the whole game. The emeralds went into the false pocket of a craftily sewn-up leather pouch. The dollars went into a plastic bag which he tied up with a giant rubber band.

He could hear a dog bark. He could hear his heart beat. He knelt down reverently before the intricately carved wooden altar, before the smiling visage of the Goddess Lakshmi, granter of boons, custodian of all wealth.

'Grant me success, Goddess Lakshmi,' he whispered. 'And ask your sister Saraswati, absent in this shrine, to grant me learning, and knowledge, and wisdom.'

There was another picture, a gilded icon of the Virgin Mary. Her smile reminded him for some reason of his mother. He crossed himself reverentially, and felt suddenly at peace with himself.

Betaab played around with the magnet and secured the door of the locker before tiptoeing out. There was a sliver of light from under one of the bedroom doors. Was the poet asleep inside?

Gently, very gently, he nudged the door open. A young woman was asleep on the bed. Her straight black hair was spread like a halo across the dishevelled pillows. A length of it cascaded onto the marble floor. Her skin was like marble too, her beautiful hands, and her feet pale and translucent covered with the faint filigree of henna flowers. She was mumbling something in her sleep, and the orbs of her closed eyes were moving, as though witnessing some celestial vision.

Betaab was transported, in his mind, in his heart, to the dark womb of a cinema hall in Kanpur, where the morning show was running his favourite film of all time, the tragic *Pakeezah*. He was inside the film, inside the frame. He was the hero Salim, he was the thespian Raaj Kumar, he was the director Kamal Amrohi.

And this languorous beauty before him, she was the courtesan Sahib Jaan, she was the tragic actress Meena Kumari, she was his muse, the muse of Urdu poetry.

Disregarding all caution, he said the lines out loud. *'Aapke paon dekhe, bahut haseen hain. Inhe zameen par mat utariyega ...maile ho jayenge.'* I saw your feet: they are beautiful. Don't place them on the ground – they will get dirty.

She heard him mumbling the lines, and slowly opened her eyes. Then went back to sleep again.

He left as he had entered, an invisible man. Raju Srivastava 'Betaab'.

Rudrani Rana, Dehradun, April

It was a warm April day in Dehradun. The ceiling fan was whirring slowly, hypnotically. Its white paint was stained and discoloured, and the blades were coated with dust.

Rudrani Rana was too tired to get up. She lay on the divan and stared at the ceiling, at the cobwebs above the slowly whirring fan. A bumblebee droned lazily by the gauze window. A lizard by the corner of the wall examined her with obsidian eyes.

She had balanced on a three-legged wooden stool in the dark bathroom and had a cold bucket-bath, then slathered herself with talcum powder before collapsing with exhaustion on the blue divan. Her black kaftan had a pattern of tiger-paws on it. A line had come to her while she was in the shower, for her new book, and she was trying to hold on to it, but the whirring fan would not let her. She could see her mother's face in the fan, changing expressions with its slow revolutions, sometimes smiling, sometimes frowning down at her.

'It was you who should have died, not your brother,' her mother was saying to her. The words had a rhythm to them, like a song, or a fierce lullaby. It-was-you-who-should-have-died-not-your-brother.

She listened patiently, waiting for her mother to disappear. The sentence in her head still awaited recording. It was slipping away.

It was almost three months since she had begun working on *Night Flashes*. Juan Torres had passed on *UNSUBMITTED* to another reader. Anirban had written to her saying he would be in contact with her, hoping to have more news soon. They would have to search for a new title, he said, as *The Face by the Window* was too similar to other recently published titles.

The new novel was a search for her father, and his forefathers. She was planning a trip to Kathmandu in May, to seek the memories of the Rana clans, to understand the journeys they had made.

Rudrani Rana was to become a rich woman soon. The land developer had strong political connections, and ever since Dehradun became the state capital of Uttarakhand, land prices had risen to unimaginable levels. Even the small share that had devolved to her would leave her comfortably well off.

Her Rana ancestors. The story had begun in 1846, after the Kot Massacre, when Jung Bahadur Rana and his brothers had murdered forty members of the Nepalese court. The long-ago Basnyat conspiracy fascinated her, and she had painstakingly worked on a novel spanning generations.

'Enough about me,' she had told herself. 'Time to move on from Rudrani Rana, from her masks and disguises. Time to go back, to retrace my DNA, to figure out where Rudrani Rana came from.'

She had begun reading up on the Ranas of Nepal. The hereditary Rana prime ministers of the Kathmandu Darbar had reduced the Shah monarchs to mere figureheads. References and background and family genealogies were there for the asking, on the net, in mildewed books in the F.R.I. Library, and through a garrulous octogenarian retired librarian she had encountered there.

Through her childhood, through her youth, Rudrani had been forbidden from so much as mentioning her father, or his family. 'It's bad blood,' she had overheard her mother say once to Stella Murch. 'Bad blood, and mad blood in their veins. It's best I continue to keep her away from that lot, as I have done.'

'Shhh,' Stella Murch had reproached. 'She mustn't hear you talk like that.' They had begun whispering to each other, and Rudrani had tiptoed past the open door, trying desperately not to think of the mad, bad blood in her veins.

There were other Rana girls in the school, all senior to her. They were all of them stunning beauties, with translucent skin, fine features and almond-shaped eyes. It was rumoured that their families were fantastically rich. Each one was escorted by a personal maid. These ayahs, in their traditional Nepalese costumes and jewellery, doubled as bodyguards. They would wait outside the wrought-iron gates all through school hours, and escort the girls home in the cars that came to pick them up.

The Rana girls had been expelled from the Waverley Girls School for smoking on the hockey field. But they had returned, triumphantly, nonchalantly, their expulsion overruled through the intervention of their rich and powerful parents.

Only now, a lifetime later and after the unexpected inheritance, did Rudrani feel the need to interrogate her famous surname, to explore her roots and heritage. She was sucked in by the excitement, the romance, the despair of that past. The privilege and licentiousness of the Rana clans who had ruled Nepal for so many centuries, and the bitter internecine intrigues between them, had taken hold of her imagination. Her ancestor, Dev Shamsher Jang Bahadur Rana, had the shortest reign in the dynasty. He had ruled for just 144 glorious days, in 1901, before he was deposed by his brothers. Known as 'The Reformist', his modern ideas and vision had been tragically thwarted by the blood feuds of his times.

After he was exiled to India, Dev Shamsher Jang Bahadur was given land by the British Raj in Jharipani, on the bridle path between Dehradun and Mussoorie. The estate was called Fairlawn. He settled there, in a magnificent Nepalese-style palace, with his twelve sons and four daughters. It was from this brood that her father, Parashuram Prajapati Rana, was descended.

Rudrani found herself immersed in Dev Shamsher's life and times, to the brief and evanescent flowering of his reign. Inspired by the Shogunate, he tried to emulate the reforms of the Meiji restoration. He imported seeds from Japan - wisteria, chrysanthemum and persimmon - and planted them across the hills and valleys of Nepal.

The exiled Rana had written to his brother pleading that he be allowed to return just once to his beloved motherland before he died. After a long silence, he received a message from the reigning prime minister which declared: *One scabbard cannot contain two swords. There is no place in Nepal for you and me.*

Broken-hearted, he had shot himself, in 1914, aged fifty-two. It was the newspaper he founded that had fascinated Rudrani most while researching Dev Shamsher's ill-documented life. *The Gorkhapatra*, which he established as a weekly in May 1901, remained to this day the national daily of Nepal. He proposed a system of universal primary education, and introduced a campaign to fight corruption. He even set up a system to fire a cannon shot at midday to announce the time.

The longer she probed, the deeper she researched, the more entranced she became with this search for her roots. It was his brother's envy that led the others to overthrow him. He had probably just been too idealistic to watch his back, she concluded pragmatically.

Too short, she thought to herself. Too short a time. And here am I, an ancient troglodyte, obsessed by my own woes, by the minor scars of an averagely hurtful childhood.

Just as her father had been, in 1950.

Many years after her mother's death, Rudrani had discovered a pistol in the locked trunk Mrs Rana kept under her bed. There were two curved knives as well - Gorkha khukris with ancient stains on them; blood or rust she could not tell.

Rudrani could still remember passing the crumbling gateway of Fairlawn as a child.

'Don't even look there,' her mother had hissed. 'That's where the rot began.'

Researching the past, recreating and reliving it, had exorcised many lingering ghosts. She felt as though her father had at last been returned to her through the history of his forefathers.

Rudrani had resolved she would visit Kathmandu only after the first draft of the book was complete. It was a partly fictionalised account, a novella really, barely forty thousand words, written in a surge of energy, a rush of discovery.

It had taken her all of four months to complete it. She had an attack of vertigo to show for her efforts. The story of Dev Shamsher Jang Bahadur Rana had come to her like a visitation. She had written it all by hand, in her neat italic handwriting, in four lined notebooks. She marvelled at how nothing had been crossed out. This time, there had been no hesitations, no question marks, no revisions.

It was, she told herself, a sort of exhumation. How could she have spent a lifetime, seven decades, knowing nothing about this past? All knowledge of the Ranas, of the seventeen brothers and their descendants, had been censored, banished, buried in hushed reprimands, by her mother.

Night Flashes had taken her out of herself, and yet, in another sense, it had restored her and given her back her sense of self.

'Perhaps there are two stories hiding within each of us,' she pondered. 'The first the story of the life we have lived, the script we have set for ourselves, and the other the "might-have-been". Or perhaps it was all the same book, chapter by chapter, between different covers. The same story, told again, from a different perspective.'

The actual process of the new book had both exhilarated and exhausted her. She had begun to see herself in a new light. The complexities of Dev Shamsher's life, the contradictions, the reversals of fortune, had explained some of her own singularities to her. She had been born to an extravagance of thought and action, which had been systematically stifled by her mother's hurts and apprehensions.

Now that Rudrani Rana had, so to say, found herself, rediscovered her core, she wondered at the person she had been. Why and how had she retreated so deeply into her own shadows?

The father she had never known, who had killed himself on her birthday. The father she had found again, after all these years. That other man, who had shamed her, who had tried to break her spirit, that man she would never name. Rupert Murch, whom she had loved, who had loved and betrayed her. His mother, her unpredictable benefactor Stella Murch, kind and cruel in equal measure. Rupert's mother, who had forbidden him from marrying Rudrani. And that monster from the past, her mother, Matron Rana, and her unspeakable words, those words that had never left her, which Rudrani had never forgotten.

'It was you who should have died, not your brother.' It-was-you-who-should-have-died-not-your-brother.

And there was her mother again, speaking in the voice of the rotating blades of the discoloured ceiling fan. Rudrani felt dizzy, and her head was spinning counter-clockwise to the movement of the fan above her. Where was she, why was she here in this unfamiliar room, sprawled upon a blue divan?

The first line from her first book. The words floated through her head, like a luminous cloud. *My body remains a haunted house.*

Then the shutdown began. First the shivering, the chilling of the bones, followed by a soft sweat that bathed her like a mist. Then the floaters, the night flashes, like meteorites and comets in a dark sky.

Then the dark, and the silence. Then a light. Her mother was waiting for her on the other side.

But she had not died. It was only a dream, or a premonition. She had slept through the day, and awoke as the last rays of the setting sun cast their grainy beams into the room.

Rudrani felt restored, renewed. She had left Dev Shamsher Jang Bahadur Rana and his reign of 144 days behind her. The crumbling balustrades of Fairlawn, the ancient bloodstains in the rusted khukris in the locked trunk under her mother's bed, the memory of her absent father - she had left these things behind, committed them to words, consigned them to the parallel space of narrative.

Only *UNSUBMITTED* remained suspended in her imagination, each word as acutely alive as when she had first written it. It was still a ghost presence in her life, her most intimate confession of herself.

My body remains a haunted house.

She missed the canvas bag, and the typed pages. Who was reading them now? Was their scrutiny understanding, and respectful? Did they get the references, the obscure jokes? Were unseen editorial eyes mocking her, and her life's work?

She registered that she was ravenously hungry. She had not eaten all day. The guest house provided only breakfast, which she had missed. She would have to walk to the canteen, or call for the chowkidar to fetch her noodles or chicken curry from a nearby dhaba.

Rudrani settled for a cup of chamomile tea, and the Marie biscuits which were kept near the electric kettle. There was an apple in her handbag. She bit into it. It was crisp and crunchy, even though the apple season was long since over. Then she felt something biting into her tongue - the cap on her front tooth had fallen off. The gap in her gums felt unfamiliar, forlorn. Perhaps she would get an implant. She could afford it now.

Rudrani decided to move into a proper hotel the next day, or perhaps into one of the tourist resorts on the road to Mussoorie. Her days of frugal living were over. There was still time. Time to travel to Rome, to Greece, the Ancient World, to eat an artichoke. Time to see the day the world would recognise her talent. Her genius.

It was dark outside. The smell of jasmine and of other fragrant night flowers wafted in from the gauze window. Through the patch of eucalyptus trees, the sounds of traffic, of speeding cars and hooting trucks. The distant barking of Bhotia dogs.

She decided to go for a walk. Leaving her handbag behind, she took just her cane and a torch to light the way through the overgrown path lined with eucalyptus trees that led to the main road. In the purple sky, she could glimpse the Pleiades, and the glimmering points of Sirius straddled across the heavens. The Dog Star. The Great Bear, pointing its way to the constant north.

And then the road, like a hungry animal, with the cars and trucks and motorcycles racing like a pack of hunting dogs. Across the road, a crescent moon, hiding among the tall branches. She stood there, undecided whether to cross the road, or to turn right, or left, or take the path back to the guest house.

The blinding headlights of a speeding truck. A motorcycle hurtling towards her like a death star. She was a football flung into the air, across the road, landing on the Lantana bushes on the other side. Her cane flew in the other direction, smashing the windshield of a scooter, but she didn't know that.

Her vision blurred. Crescent moons spread in an arc across the sky. Darkness crept through her skull like advancing night.

The police found her the next morning, an aged woman with no markers of identity on her. It took two days for the guest house to report her missing. Her body lay in the mortuary until the chowkidar came forward to identify her.

They could not trace her next of kin, but the land deeds and legal correspondence led the police to the lawyer who was handling her case. He informed them of her last will and testament, naming Anirban M. as the sole heir to her now considerable fortune.

The news of Rudrani Rana's death hit Anirban more deeply than he could have ever anticipated. It seemed to establish, finally and incontrovertibly, the futility and horror of things.

But there was her book, a testament to her grit, the record and residue of her Unsubmittable spirit.

It seemed inconceivable that Rudrani had named him her heir, that the chance meeting in the press terrace had linked him so irrevocably to her. He was to fly to Barcelona the day he received the news, for a workshop, and then a week of travel with Juan Torres. He cancelled his ticket, postponed his trip. It seemed callous and uncaring to spend no time mourning her.

There was no ritual of grief he could turn to; there was no one to console, or share memories with. He had the charcoal portrait he had drawn framed in gold; he placed it on his desk, next to the original typed manuscript of *UNSUBMITTED*, nestling in its canvas tote bag. He hunted through all the florist shops in search of purple flowers, but could find nothing apart from two stems of mauve and maroon gladioli. He placed the flowers in a long-stemmed vase, lit a patchouli candle, and recited the Gayatri mantra.

> 'Lead us from darkness to light
> From death to immortality.'

Then he played some organ music which he downloaded from the net, poured himself a drink, and wept.

Anura, Bangalore, later

Schoolgirl Anura was working on her new novel. 'How and where do you stop telling a story?' she wondered. 'How and when do you give it the sense of an ending?'

Her mother had made her promise to stop writing. 'Just for the next few years, Anuradha, until the Boards are over and we get you into college. These are the most important years of your life. You can scribble away all you want after that, darling, but right now you have to cram. To ingest, remember and retain. It's a competitive world out there, a cruel world, and we want our only daughter to be not just a survivor, but a winner!'

Anura despised her mother. Her father was nice, but completely in his wife's control. He gave in to everything, to organic food, meditation weekends, sessions at the gym. Her mother believed that a family was a unit, and that the three of them, plus a Golden Retriever, were never happier than when doing things together.

She had made her private escape through books. First reading, and then writing. She was working on her third novel now. It was titled *The Revenge of the Reptiles*.

Her mother knew nothing about her. Parents never did. Although she was an only child, her mother always alluded to her as their 'only daughter'. This puzzled her, troubled her inordinately.

'My only daughter has written a book,' the woman would mention casually, with a bright smile accentuated by her bright lipstick. She often tapped her long oval nails, also painted in bright colours, on a nearby surface - a table, a glass, the wooden armrest of a chair - to emphasise what she was saying.

'My only daughter has written - and published - two books.' It was as though Anura didn't have a name, as though she was born to be the daughter who was part of the eternal quartet of the husband, the dog, and of course, the mother. The boastful tone in which she talked about Anura's books seemed almost to indicate that it was she, in her inner inspirational and supervisory capacity, who had driven her 'only daughter' to such a worthy enterprise.

It made Anura want to puke. She felt trapped in her genetic family, although she was fond of the Golden Retriever. In her inevitable Harry Potter phase, she had decided her parents were in fact Muggles, concealing her true magical ancestry from her. But her obsession soon moved from Potter to J.K. Rowling herself. That was her destiny - to have a net worth of billions, to be richer than the Queen of England, and more famous. That was the power of words.

Her new book was about artificial intelligence and the narratives of the future. The idea had come to her on the train to Jaipur, the year she had gone there to speak. Speculative fiction was quite different from magic and fantasy: it was the genre of the future, of *her* future. She had begun writing systematically to literary agents around the world, from an alphabetical index she had compiled. Very few replied. She had filed all their rejections in a folder titled UNDEAD, and spat out an arcane voodoo curse on them while clicking save. The dark arts were alive on the internet, and there was always something to learn.

Tomorrow is waiting. That was how her new book began. It was about a manic depressive AI researcher who was working on king cobras and their photographic memories. The researcher was a third-gender mutant, whose mother had died of snakebite. The story got complicated after that, and Anura was still trying to sort out some contradictory strands.

The theme was revenge. As the snake memory metamorphosed into artificial biomes, it carried the imprint of hurt and abuse by the human race.

Elephants had photographic memories too. Matriarch elephants remembered things in the deep past, and guided their extended herd communities with the accumulated wisdom of their stories and recollections.

Anura was considering the idea of working an elephant into her narrative, but it would, she thought on balance, disturb if not destroy the structure of the narrative.

'Stories need to have a shape,' she noted, and put it up as a pinned tweet in her Twitter account.

Meanwhile, she had to get down to writing an essay for a school project. On 'Abraham Lincoln and Mahatma Gandhi'. She looked it all up on the net and came up with a few well-tweaked sentences. *Abraham Lincoln and Mohandas Karamchand Gandhi, the two towering personalities of the nineteenth and twentieth centuries, were a study in contrasts.*

Oh, the tedium of being a schoolchild. She could hear soft sounds of music from the living room. Leaving Lincoln and Gandhi halfway, she found her father sitting in his favourite rocking chair, twanging a guitar.

Anura didn't betray her surprise. She raised an eyebrow interrogatively, and let the hint of a smile escape to indicate her approval.

Dad gave her a contented smile back. 'I used to play the guitar in school,' he said happily. 'I thought I would pick up the threads again - I mean the strings.'

She was glad for him. The old were another country. Or another species. But there was always scope for human evolution, or any evolution. It could run backwards or forwards or in any direction at all.

She decided to go to the mall for a break. She liked to be among crowds of people; it made her feel more alone, more special. Besides, she didn't want to wallow in Beatles nostalgia with her dad. Mother might even decide to sing along. Best to escape.

A new bookstore had opened recently on the seventh floor of the mall. It was more a coffee shop than a bookshop, really. *Browse our bookshelves with a cup of cappuccino.* That's what their posters said. Anura's favourite bookstore had a second-hand section which smelt of damp and secrets and forgotten mysteries. She had actually discovered a signed copy of a V.S. Naipaul novel there, tucked among a heap of old books. But there was something enticing about the new bookstore, where the smell of coffee mixed and blended with the fragrance of books.

The week's bestsellers were displayed in the glass window by the entrance. One of the covers stood out from all the others. It had a pencil and charcoal drawing of an old woman, a woman with fine, sculpted features and a slight hunch. Something about the unravelling bun, the trailing shawl, unlocked a forgotten memory. There were two handbags on the table before her, one an everyday leather handbag, the other an oversized tote bag.

The title was embossed in gold and purple, in capital letters. *UNSUBMITTED* by Rudrani Rana.

It was the woman on the train. Farhan and she had been on their way to the literature festival. She had made up an elaborate fantasy game, she couldn't remember what …

She asked for the book and examined it with all the care of an archaeologist studying an artefact chanced upon during an excavation. She turned it this way and that, the spine, the font, the number of pages.

It was a hardback edition, priced at Rs 799.

Cover illustration by Anirban M.

The magnum opus of a magnificent and original writer, whose genius was discovered tragically too late.

The bio note on the back flap was quite minimal. *Rudrani Rana was born in Dehradun in 1949. She died in 2017.* UNSUBMITTED *has been published to much posthumous advance praise.*

Anura didn't like the construction of that sentence. 'Published to much posthumous advance praise.' It needed an edit.

Funds were low. She would buy the book with next month's pocket money.

Examinations were looming, and she had to carry on labouring surreptitiously on *The Revenge of the Reptiles*. She couldn't afford to get distracted. She would read *UNSUBMITTED* next month.

'Rudrani Rana,' she said out loud, testing the words on her tongue. It was a good name for an author. The woman on the train.

Her mind returned, inevitably, to her own book, the one she was writing. Tomorrow is waiting, she thought to herself.

Anirban M. was tearing up his notebooks. Something had descended upon him, like a cloud. Was it rage? Anger? Passion? No, it was rather an overwhelming sense of futility.

In every cupboard, in every room, in every life, there are unnecessary, unused objects and emotions we don't know what to do with. There were sheets and notebooks and torn-off pages from drawing pads piled around in every corner of his studio. Every artist in the world has his or her own peculiar mode of disorder, a secret code of blind memory. He, and he alone, knew where those stacked-up images, current and discarded, were kept, and why. Of course there were some surprises, and discoveries, but these did not move him.

At first he shredded them into long strips, and piled them into the centre of the room, on the cracked terrazzo floor. Then he worked on them again, creating an abstract fugue-like pattern. He examined his handiwork with satisfaction before he got to stoking his rage again, stamping on the papers, kicking them around with Russian dance moves and Cossack footwork. He then set to tearing them up again, into smaller and yet smaller pieces. The fragments of his drawings lay around him, runes in a cryptic hieroglyphic script. Anirban began rearranging them yet again into whimsical formations, in a scattered circle, before tiptoeing away so as not to disturb the pattern.

He switched on the ceiling fan and began fiddling about with the regulator. Speed One. Two. Three. Four. *Five.* The papers flew around in a mad frenzy before drifting into different corners of the room, sheltering under chairs, hiding under tables, cowering under the bookshelf.

He felt calmer now, renewed and ready to face life and work and deadlines and lunch with his cousin Chintan Banerjea, who was making overtures of friendship after his appointment as the editor of a leading economic newspaper.

Chintan had offered Anirban a weekly column. It was to be titled *Vexations* and feature what Chintan had called a 'visuals and text combo'. The phrase had both repelled and intrigued Anirban, but that, he philosophised, was the nature of the marketplace.

Juan Torres was slipping out of his life. He had taken off to a retreat in Nepal for a spiritual self-help course. Anirban had wanted to join him, but had received an ambiguous email in reply. 'There is too much passion, too much intensity, and also too much distance between us. The magnetism, the *duende*, is complicated by too many other things. It's best at this point that I go there alone.'

What were 'the other things'? The very thought of Juan stirred him up again. He began searching for more papers to destroy, more memories to tear up. His eyes fell on the spiral-bound Jaipur notebook. He started to leaf through it, impatiently, anxiously, scanning each page to see what recollections it dredged up.

A woman with a mane of grey shaded hair looked back at him questioningly. Who was she? He checked his notes on the adjoining page. Zoya Mankotia. Of course he remembered her. He had sketched her for the *Faces of the Festival* series. He remembered her unusual, intriguing face and the cascade of jasper-coloured hair.

Zoya had shown him the anonymous letter she had received, and the pretty purple envelope with the pussycat card inside. She had been hurt and puzzled, but he had recognised the sender, realised it was Rudrani Rana, recognised *her* hurt and pain. Even in those early days, he had sided with her, kept her secrets, defended her in his heart.

He continued turning the pages, although he knew he was getting late for lunch. Gayatri Gandhy. She had a face that didn't give much away. Pretty, poised, on her guard, she could be anybody. He had liked her, enjoyed her company. He would email her to see how she was getting along. And there was Juan, heartbreakingly handsome, one of Anirban's early sketches of him. There had been so many more, many of them lying in shreds and tatters around him. His esteemed cousin, Chintan Banerjea, with his own dramatic streak of grey hair. Chintan would be waiting for him; it was time for him to leave for lunch.

He had drawn Rudrani Rana, in that first portrait on the press terrace at the festival. He couldn't find it, until he remembered he had removed it from the folio for the cover of *UNSUBMITTED*.

The book. The canvas bag. These things remained of her. He had placed five copies of her novel, her published novel, in her canvas bag, a sort of shrine to her memory. A tribute to poison-pen letters, to truth-tellers, to those who struggled and persisted to tell their stories. If only she had lived to hold the book, to see her words in print.

It was in the nature of things that the young did not, could not, understand the fragility of time. He went online to search a ticket for Nepal. Chintan would understand; lunch could wait for a while.

GRATITUDE

To my co-director William Dalrymple, to Sanjoy Roy and all the extended family of readers and writers who helped create this festival which spreads so much joy. Thank you, Rosemarie Hudson and HopeRoad, for the love and care you gave this book. To Joan Deitch for the thoughtful edits, and James Nunn for the delightful cover. To all the characters who wandered into these pages, to Rudrani Rana, to Anura, to Anirban, Raju Srivastava 'Betaab', and to all of you, gratitude for sharing your stories.

Namita Gokhale, founder-director of the vibrant Jaipur Literature Festival, is herself a publisher and the acclaimed author of twenty books. Both non-fiction and fiction, they include the best-selling *Paro: Dreams of Passion*, *Priya*, and *Things to Leave Behind*.

In 2017 Namita was awarded the first ever Centenary National Award for Literature by the Literary Society of Assam for her service to the Indian nation in supporting and showcasing Indian writing talents and creating a literary environment in the country. She has been described as one of the finest Indian writers.

Namita Gokhale lives in New Delhi.